An Incident at the Devil's Tramping Ground
A Novel By

Stanley D. Ivie

*To Martha
A life long friend
Stan Ivie*

An Incident at the Devil's Tramping Ground

Copyright © 2022 by Stanley D. Ivie

Printed in the United States of America. All rights reserved.

ISBN 9798797688433

An Incident at the Devil's Tramping Ground

A Novel

By

Stanley D. Ivie

Biographical Sketch

Stanley D. Ivie is Professor Emeritus from Texas Woman's University. He is an established scholar, having published 60 some articles in prestige journals. He is also the author of a textbook, *On the Wings of Metaphor*, and a novel, *In the Shadow of the Trojan Horse*. Professor Ivie retired from active teaching in 2007. He moved to a ranch in Southern Utah were he designed and built a house largely with his own labor. He currently resides on his ranch with his wife, Jeri; their dog, Bonto; one horse, Ace; four cats; and a hummingbird who returns every spring.

Dedicated to Jeri, Lanette, and Lindsay without whose help this novel would not have been possible.

And the fifth angel blew his trumpet,

and I saw a star fallen from heaven to

earth, and he was given the key to the

shaft of the bottomless pit.

Revelations

Preface

Hidden among the dark pines of the North Carolina Piedmont there is a place—an unearthly place—a patch of soil where nothing grows—a barren spot formed in the shape of a perfect circle. The people of the region know this place as the Devil's Tramping Ground. As legend would have it, Satan appears there when the moon is full—walks the outer parameter of the circle—walks and broods—plots and schemes—works his vengeance against the world.

Chapters

Chapter 1 The Chase   8

Chapter 2 The Family   28

Chapter 3 The University   105

Chapter 4 The Maelstrom   173

Chapter 1

The Chase

She fled into the gathering darkness—baby clutched tightly against her swollen breasts. A fallen branch snaps—cracks under foot—shattering the frozen silence of the darkening woods. The wind—harsh—cruel—whistling through the lonely pines. The moon—fat—gloated—ringed with a malevolent glow—peeking down upon a frantic flight. The scurry of orange-brown leaves across the windswept path. Short bursts of pained breath becoming quickened. The distant barking of dogs—having picked up the scent of a frightened prey.

The chase—the hunter and the hunted—the pursuer and the pursued—roles forever changing—forever remaining the same. But for this moment—this finite speck of time—the roles are cast. What chance a fawn—legs not come to full quickness—to elude a snarling pack? Holly branches reach out—greedily slashing soft flesh—staining its leaves to match its berries. The heart becomes a throbbing demon—pounding against its captive walls. Flashing lights of fear—tender yellows, intense reds, wondering blues—all melt into the opaque glaze of tear-swollen eyes.

On the far off Serengeti plains a pride of young lions snarl and rip at the open bowels of a fallen gazelle. In the Sea of Japan, shark's teeth cut and slash at the bleeding belly of a baby whale. High over the Arizona desert an eagle circles—spreading its talons as it swoops down upon an unsuspecting rabbit. An age-old story plays out its familiar restrains.

The pace quickens. The barking becomes louder, closer. Scurrying feet slip on frozen mud. A large root—prominently enthroned upon the ground—catches fast an ankle—smiles as it hears a bone snap. Swirling darkness rushes in—engulfing the fallen prey. Pain! Terror! Abandonment! The muffled cry of a new born baby spilled from its mother's protective arms.

....

The Reverend Andrew Godfrey, loyal servant of God and kindly shepherd of his flock, was in a jovial mood. He had eaten well, and after eating he enjoyed engaging in a bit of light conversation. He liked to talk—reveled in the sound of words—their rhythmic rise and fall—the way they slipped off his tongue. Easing his chair away from the dinner table, he looked at his wife and said, "Excellent venison, my dear, really superb."

"Why thank you Andrew. I prepared it the way you always like—plenty of garlic and peppercorns."

Martha Godfrey was a comely woman in her early

fifties. She had married while still a girl, barely fifteen. She had given her husband five sons—only two of whom were still living. Her life as the wife of an Anglican Minister living on the North Carolina frontier had not been an easy one. Here, on the edge of civilization, everyday was a struggle. Her household chores always began at dawn— meals to prepare, dishes to wash, clothes to mend, a garden to tend. Martha knew the meaning of hard work, but she never complained. She accepted her lot in life. She knew no other.

"Yes, it really was a delicious meal." The words came from Herman Schertz, who was a Lutheran from the German settlement at Salem. Herman was returning from the trip to Raleigh where he had made the acquaintance of Howard Godfrey, the Reverends younger brother. Howard had asked him to deliver a letter to his brother on his way back to Salem. Herman had accepted the responsibility. When he had arrived at Reverend Godfrey's home, it was just in time for dinner. The Reverend, pleased to have word from his brother, had invited Herman to share in the hospitality of his table.

"I wish though," the Reverend continued, "we'd had a spot of currant jelly to go with the venison. It would have added immeasurably to the flavor of the meal."

"I'm sorry Andrew, but you finished what little we had last week. The bushes last year were very light."

The Reverend frowned, added, "Well perhaps you could speak with Henry George's wife. They always seem to have plenty of currant jelly. I know Henry has jelly with his venison. His eight little ruffians have currant jelly with their venison. I'll wager even Henry's mangy dogs have currant jelly with their venison. Everyone in this parish has currant jelly except the minister. These people have too little fear of God. They have all forgotten how to tithe. Give a Crown to Jesus! Crown! I would settle for a shilling!" A smile crept around the corners of the

Reverend's mouth. "That would make a fine sermon, Less Clowning and More Crowning."

Herman laughed at the Reverend's play on words. "I can see why they all say you're the most popular preacher in North Carolina. I wish I could stay to attend one of your sermons."

"There is no reason to rush off," the Reverend assured him. "Let's move in by the fireplace. Martha can bring us a spot of tea."

The two men stood and walked into the living room. The Reverend poked the coals in the fire—tossing on another log before settling back into his well-worn rocking chair. Herman seated himself on a high-backed chair across from the Reverend's.

The Reverend picked up a long-stemmed pipe with a porcelain bowl and began packing it with tobacco. "Can I offer you some of my tobacco? We grow and cure it ourselves. We are lucky to live in North Carolina. We grow the finest tobacco in the colonies."

"No, I'm afraid I have never acquired the habit."

"Is that right? I didn't think there was a man in the colonies who hadn't acquired the habit of smoking. The Indians claim it will cure whatever ails you—rheumatism, the gout, even diarrhea." The Reverend paused while lighting his pipe. Then he added, "I shot the doe we had for dinner. She was standing quietly down by the creek. It was quite a choir dragging her back up to the barn. But if you like venison, that's what you've got to do."

"It really made for a fine meal," Herman confirmed.

The Reverend puffed on his pipe for several minutes in silence, savoring the rich aroma of his tobacco. Then, removing the pipe from his mouth, he turned and addressed his guest. "Herman, it was good of you to bring the letter from my brother. I rarely get to see him anymore. It is a long journey from here to Raleigh. I must tell you, I find his words distressing. He is a Wig—you know—taking up arms against the Crown. Revolution! That is all he can talk about. He wants me to come and join him—me—a minister of God."

"I take it you're a Loyalist."

"No, no, I didn't say that. I haven't taken sides—though God knows I have prayed enough about it. All the confusion—turmoil—lack of order—I find the whole nasty business to be very distressing."

"My people share in your concern. We've lived many years in this colony in peace. Why destroy all we've gained. There is much apprehension about the news coming from Boston. Surely the Sons of Liberty can't mean to take on the might of the whole British army?"

"I'm afraid that's exactly what they intend. My brother writes that it is now impossible to reconcile the differences between the Crown and the colonies. A fellow by the name of Thomas Paine has written a pamphlet,

Common Sense. According to Howard, it is being read by every patriot in the colonies. Paine has posed a very important question: Should a continent be ruled by an island? I am told Mr. Jefferson from Virginia has written a document they are calling The Declaration of Independence. I am afraid nothing good is going to come of all of this."

Martha arrived at the doorway to the living room. She had a tray containing a pot of hot tea and two cups.

The Reverend looked up, smiled, said, "Oh, thank you my dear. A cup of hot tea is just what we need on an evening like this."

Martha placed the silver tea service on a small table next to her husband's rocking chair. She poured a cup for their guest and another for her husband. Having performed her wifely duties, she returned to the kitchen—leaving the two men alone to finish solving the problems of the world.

17

"Revolution!" the Reverend said reflectively. "I hope the whole sordid business can be settled peacefully. War is an abomination in the eyes of God. It is the most surefire way I know of destroying church attendance. You mark my word."

Suddenly there was a loud knocking on the front door. The Reverend looked taken back—surprised to hear someone at his door in the dark of night. He sat down his cup of tea and went to see who was making such a racket.

Opening the door he saw the frost-bitten face of his neighbor, John Harvey, who looked as though he had been running and was about to collapse from exhaustion. Before the Reverend could invite him in to warm himself, John blurted out, "It's happened—come quickly—she's had her baby!"

"So she's had her baby," the Reverend confirmed. "Saddle my horse. No, better make it two horses." Glancing at Herman he added, "You're going to want to come along—see this for yourself. Looking toward the kitchen he

called, "Martha, my Bible and Holy Water, please!"

. . . .

Tall graceful pines looked placidly down upon the

scene unfolding at their feet. A handful of men—good,

honest, God-fearing men—were gathered around a small

bonfire—trying to warm themselves against the cold.

Barking dogs tugging at their leashes—eager to resume the

chase. The figure of a young woman was sprawled upon

the frozen ground—a tattered blue shawl wrapped

protectively around her infant.

Some things never change—mother and child—

nature and nurture—little possums enveloped in a velvety-

soft pouch—baby birds crowded tightly together in a

downy-filled nest—puppies stacked upon one another in a

furry-warm heap—an infant wrapped in swaddling clothes—soft—warm—protected.

The men looked up from the fire to witness two horses approaching. Several dogs stood erect—sniffing the air—beginning a mournful howl. A tall, lanky man left the fire—catching the reins of one of the horses as it enters the clearing—announced: "Glad you could make it Reverend— waited for you—glad you're here—wouldn't know what to do without you."

"Well, Henry," the Reverend replied, dismounting from his horse, "you might remember to express those sentiments to your good wife the next time she is wondering what to do with all of her fine currant jelly."

Reverend Godfrey walked to where the fire was burning—warming his hands—greeting the men who were gathered there. "Hellish night to be out—eh boys?"

Several men nodded—muttering about the cold.

Herman Schertz—having wrapped his horse's reins around a small sapling—joined the other men around the fire.

"Boys," the Reverend began, "I'd like you to meet Mr. Schertz. He lives over at Salem—was good enough to bring me a letter from my brother from Raleigh. I thought he'd want to see this business for himself."

There was an exchange of mumbled names and a clasping of frozen hands.

Henry George—having taken care of the Reverend's horse—joined the other men around the bonfire. "Glad you're here Reverend," he said, repeating his words from earlier. "We wouldn't know what to do without you. None of us have had any experience with this sort of thing."

The Reverend looked at the sullen faces gathered around the fire, said thoughtfully: "God calls each of us to serve His purposes in different ways."

"Is that the woman?" Herman asked, motioning toward the crumpled figure lying on the ground at the far side of the clearing.

"Yes," the Reverend replied.

"And you say she's a witch!"

"No doubt about it—right boys?"

A chorus of yeas and curses came from the other men.

She's got the mark of witch all right," Henry George confirmed. "I saw it with my own eyes. Last spring I was down at the river fishing. She came along and stood on the bank—not more than fifty yards away. She didn't know I was there—had my back up against a big tree. Pretty soon she takes off all her clothes—shameless witch—and jumps into the river. She stayed there for the longest time—as if she knew she wouldn't drown. When she got out—that's when I saw it—the mark of Satan on her breast."

The other men nodded—having heard Henry's story for the umpteenth time.

"She's a witch—no doubt about it," the Reverend confirmed. "She'd like nothing better than to go on practicing her black magic right here under our noses. Thought she could have her baby without our taking notice—use its blood—un-baptized blood—in one of her devilish rituals. Well, we intend to put a stop to all of her Satanism right here and now!" He looked across the dancing flames at the frozen figure lying on the ground. Quoting from Exodus he added in a voice of righteous indignation: "Thou shall not suffer a witch to live."

A gray owl flew across the face of the moon—landing on a branch looking down upon the clearing. "Hoo," the bird asked? "Hoo" is the woman lying prostrated on the ground? "Hoo" are these men gathered around the fire? "Hoo" invited them into my woods? "Hoo" authorized these proceedings?

"Hadn't we better get on with it? Herman asked.

"Yes, I guess we should at that," the Reverend replied, still warming his hands against the cold.

Herman left the fire and walked to where the crumpled body of a woman was lying. He was followed by the Reverend, Henry George, and several other men. They stood—looking at the pathetic figure at their feet. Her face and arms had been scratched red by the Holly Bushes. Her dress was torn and soaked with frozen blood. She appeared to be more dead than alive.

"She hemorrhaged during the chase," Henry George offered. "That's how we were able to follow her tracks."

The Reverend bent down over the fallen prey. Suddenly dark eyes flashed upward—meeting his own. "There, there, my child," he said, using his most pastoral voice. We mean you no harm. All we want—all we have come for is the baby."

A weak voice—barely audible—replied: "You can't have him. He's mine."

"We mean you no harm," the Reverend repeated, but this time with a more assertive quality in his voice. "I've promised my congregation to put an end to witchcraft, and by all that is Holy I intend to do just that! We are all decent, God-fearing people. We intend to make this land fit for our women and children. We've had quite enough of your Satan worship."

"She's a witch all right," Henry George asserted, "I saw her mark myself. I say we put an end to her right here and now."

Several other men echoed the same sentiment.

"Fools," she hissed, hollow eyes turned accusingly toward Henry George, who turned and looked back toward the fire.

At just that moment the Reverend reached down and snatched the bundle from the woman's weakened arms.

"Fools! Hypocrites!" She shrieked with her dying breath. "So I'm a witch. All right! I curse all of you! May your children and grandchildren carry my curse until the seventh generation." Then, coughing up blood, she fell back on the ground—eyes turning inward. The womb that had given birth spilled its last drops of blood on the ground.

"What should we do with her?" Herman asked.

"We'll have to dig a hole and bury her," the Reverend replied, still holding the whimpering bundle in his arms.

"We didn't bring a shovel," Henry George said apologetically. "We'll need a pickax in order to break through the frozen layer of earth."

"All right," the Reverend said, "fetch me my saddle bags and the horse blanket. We'll use the blanket to cover her body until we can get back here in the morning with a pick and shovel. Does anyone have a better idea?"

The men shook their heads, muttering a strong number of nos.

Henry George returned with the Reverend's saddle bags and the horse blanket. The Reverend took the saddle bags and motioned for Henry to place the blanket over the body on the ground. Taking a flask of Holy Water from one side of the saddlebags, he unfastened the lid, dipping in two fingers and sprinkling a few drops on the exposed brow of the infant. Then, raising his eyes toward heaven, he said in his most pontifical voice: "Lord we beseech Thee to open Thy Arms to this little lost soul!"

"What are you going to name him?" Henry asked.

The Reverend gave Henry George a knowing look and replied: "We'll name him George Henry Godfrey—and touching the Holy Water for a second time to the child's brow added: "I christen thee George Henry Godfrey in the name of the Father, the Son, and the Holy Ghost."

Suddenly, a blast of wind caught the fire and sent a shower of sparks flying in all directions. The dogs began to howl—the horses pulled at their reins—a shooting star fell from the heavens—the ground under the men's feet shook—and the owl took to flight—hooting as it flew away—"hoo, hoo, hoo" was given the key to the bottomless pit?

Chapter 2

The Family

"Oh, no, Mother!" The dust—the scattered newspapers—the cigar filled ashtray—the breakfast dishes—all joined in the same chorus—caught, Jennifer, you're caught!

Jennifer scooped up the yellow cat, which had been sleeping on the sofa, and dropped it on the floor. She made a frenzied dash to gather up the newspapers—to dump the ashtray—to hide the breakfast dishes in the sink. Then, giving the living room a final disparaging look, she opened the front door.

"Well, hey, Mom, Dad—I didn't know you were going to drop by."

"It was such a lovely day—thought we'd take a drive—bring you some flowers from the garden—see our little grandson," the words were those of Grace Godfrey Charleston.

Grace handed her daughter a small bouquet of daffodils while her blue-gray eyes scanned the efficiency apartment. The gray carpet—not beyond hope. The stench of stale cigar smoke—she would marry a man who smoked. What a filthy habit—not good for the baby. The blue velvet sofa and chair she had given them as a wedding gift— seemingly converted into a soiled clothes hamper. Messy! Simply messy! How could she—a member of the Charleston family—live like this? After all she had tried to teach her daughter southern etiquette—given her piano lessons—White Grove School—and this was the thanks she received. She had wanted to give her daughter a proper wedding, but no she had to run off and married one of those people—not even a Christian!

How have you been, Dad?" Jennifer asked, giving her father an affectionate look.

"Oh, your mother and I have been just fine."

"And how have you all been, my dear, and where is Jules?" Grace asked, cutting short her husband's conversation with his daughter.

"Jules, well, he went over to the library to . . . ."

"And where is my little grandson? And, oh yes, I almost forgot. Mrs. Graham stopped us on the way out of church—asked to be remembered. You must have her over for tea, soon. She's so anxious to see the baby. Poor thing, her own grandchildren are way off in Oregon."

"Chucky is taking a nap. He should be awake anytime—can I get you anything—a cup of coffee?"

"Oh, goodness me no. After church we stopped by the Colonial Inn—had a simply fabulous meal—fried chicken with all the trimmings. You should try eating there sometime, my dear. You loved it so much when you were a little girl."

"Jules is so busy with his studies that we rarely go out to eat anymore."

"Dear," Grace said, scanning her daughter's appearance, "you are beginning to look dowdy. I have discovered the most wonderful spa. It's simply marvelous. Why don't you come with me next week? Your father would be happy to buy you a membership. Wouldn't you dear?"

Charles Charleston, a quiet-eyed man in his mid-fifties, nodded his agreement.

"A woman has to watch her figure—especially after she's had a baby." Grace paused for a moment—pressing her fingers against her stomach. "I can still wear my wedding dress."

A look of hurt crept across Jennifer's face. "Maybe I could when Jules finishes his degree. I'm trying to help him. What with the typing and the baby, I don't see how I could do that right now."

"Oh, yes, working your fingers to the bone. Did I tell you Ella has a new maid—says she is simply wonderful. Why don't you let your daddy hire a maid for you—send her over two days a week—a little Mother's Day present? You would be happy to do that, wouldn't you dear?"

"I don't know, Jules says . . . ."

"Oh, I think I hear our little grandson now," Grace said, cocking her head to one side.

"He probably needs to be changed," Jennifer replied, walking toward the bedroom.

"Charles," Grace whispered to her husband, "we've simply have to get her some help. Look at this apartment! No one in our family has ever lived like this."

Charles passively nodded his head in agreement.

"And look at your daughter. She was such a pretty girl. Maybe she'll listen to you. She was always a daddy's girl."

Jennifer reappeared with a one-year-old baby boy in her arms.

"Oh, there he is," Grace exclaimed, taking the baby from his mother's arms. "And look at you—haven't you grown. Oh, Charles, see how he smiles. He loves his grandmother." She pressed the baby tightly against her breasts.

Charles smiled—reaching out and patting the baby on the head. "He certainly is a Charleston—look at those legs—going to be a quarterback for Duke."

"Jules says he wants him to be a scholar."

"By the way, Jennifer," Grace added, rocking the baby back and forth in her arms, "Reverend Blake asked us to send his regards—wanted to know when you're going to have the baby christened? Aunt Ella and the Norton's both want to come by. You shouldn't put things off, my dear."

Just then the front door sprang open. Jules Stein, a dark complexioned man in his mid-thirties, stood in the opening, a half-smoked cigar in his mouth. Jules' eyes quickly read the faces starring back at him. He gave his mother-in-law a knowing smile and nodded respectfully at her father. Then, walking over to where his wife was standing, he gave her a quick kiss on the cheek, asked, "Have you finished with my typing?"

"Typing?" Jennifer looked caught off guard. "I haven't had a chance—mother—Chucky."

Jules gave his wife a disapproving look, added: "You know I have to have a draft finished by tomorrow."

"I know, I'm sorry, I'll try getting to it this evening."

"What are you writing?" Grace asked, having seated herself on the sofa where she was bouncing Chucky lightly on her lap.

"Superstition."

"Oh, yes, I'm sure you must find it all very interesting—devils and witches and all of that. Jennifer had an ancestor, a minister, one of the early settlers in this part of the state, who helped to burn a witch."

"Oh, mother, they didn't actually burn her."

"They did so. Didn't they Charles?" Grace did not like being contradicted, least of all by her daughter. "It says they burned her in our old family Bible."

"I don't believe it actually says they burned her," Charles said, entering the conversation. "It seems to me they just ran her out of town, though I could be wrong about that. It has been a long time since I read those old letters stuck in the back of your great, great, grandfather's Bible."

"Well, I remember perfectly well," Grace retorted. "And they burned her someplace out in the woods."

Jules was suddenly interested in the story. "I'd like to take a look at those old letters sometime. It might prove useful in my research."

"They are all out at the farm—up in the attic in an old trunk. Jennifer can take you there. She knows what I'm talking about. When she was a little girl, she used to love to play hide-and-seek in the attic." Charles glancing at his daughter, added, "Be sure to give Addie a call before you go. Let her know you're coming."

Jules gave his wife a questioning look—as if to ask who is Addie?

"Oh, you've never met Addie," Jennifer said. "She's been with our family for a long, long time. She lives out at the farm—looks after the old place. She's a little strange but very nice."

A smile crossed Jules' face. "Just think—witchcraft right here in the family."

"Oh, Jules," Jennifer protested.

"We were just telling Jennifer how everyone at church was asking about the baby, Chucky," Grace said, switching the topic of conversation. "I'm sure you'd both have enjoyed Reverend Blake's sermon. He talked about—Charles—what was it he talked about?"

"The error we make in following non-Christian religions like the Mormons and the Jehovah Witnesses."

"Of course, we don't believe any of their kind of non-sense. Our family has always been Episcopalian. We don't have any silly beliefs."

"Oh, really, what about Virgin Birth? How did God pull off that trick?" Jules asked, a cutting quality in his voice.

An icy silence settled over the room.

"We really must be going," Grace said, coming to her feet and passing Chucky back to his mother. "I told Charles earlier I wanted to stop by the mall."

"You don't have to rush off," Jennifer protested.

"It's time we were going." Grace's eyes made a final sweeping survey of her daughter's apartment before adding: "Call me tomorrow. We really must get you some help."

....

The earth was alive with the signs of spring. The recent rains had left the red clay soil of the North Carolina Piedmont rich and moist. Lacy-white dogwoods dotted the landscape, accentuating the virgin green of the forest. The air was rife with the scent of flowers—red tulips, yellow daffodils, blue pansies—drifting out from the garden and across the lawn where several shirtless young men were tossing a Frisbee. The afternoon sun was deliciously warm, framed against a hazy-blue sky. Life was one with itself, growth and renewal.

Chucky Stein was one with life. When he awakened from his afternoon nap, his mother had feed him lunch and dressed him in his navy-blue sailor's suit. She had wrapped him in his favorite blanket with the bunnies and baby chicks woven into its fabric. The two of them set off for a walk with the stroller. Their short walk brought them to Duke University's Garden. Now—at this very moment— Chucky was lying on his blanket—kicking, smiling, reaching for his toes. His chubby little legs caught the rays of the sun—giving off a warm, healthy glow. Chucky Stein was loved, and he knew it.

"Sorry I'm late," Jules said, hurrying up to where his wife and son were seated on the grass. "Have you been waiting long?"

"No, we just arrived—were enjoying the sun."

Jules joined his family on the blanket. "I thought I'd be finished in the library before now—wanted to run over my notes one last time. Prelims! Lord, I'll be glad when their finished."

Jules rolled over and placed his mouth on his son's tummy—blowing and making a buzzing sound. Chucky smiled—squirmed—delighted at his father's attention.

"Say, look at this kid. He is getting pretty husky. What have you been feeding him?"

Jennifer smiled warmly, replied, "Split peas and macaroni." She was happy to see her husband taking an interest in their son. He was usually so absorbed in his school work he would completely forget about his family. She had always wanted a family—to have a baby—to be a loving mother. What was life without love? Of course there were days—days when cooking, dishes, and laundry all piled up on her—days when she wished she could change her name and run away and hide. But then there were good

41

days too—days like today—days when it was good just to be alive.

"Mother called," Jennifer offered hesitantly. "She is still upset about the other day. I wish you wouldn't argue with her. You know how it makes me feel."

"Oh, all right, I'm sorry." Jules rolled over and looked up at the sky. "You know how hard it is to resist saying something about all of the non-sense that comes out of her mouth. She is always setting herself up."

"I know, but that's just her way. She's not going to change. When your father was here, I didn't treat him like that."

"He isn't the dingdong you're mother is."

Jennifer's face registered a hurt look. "I really wish you'd try."

Jules rolled over to where his wife was lying on the blanket—taking her hand and giving it a little kiss. "Okay,

I'll try not to listen to what your mother has to say when she comes around. That is probably the best I can do."

Chucky, who had been lying quietly on the blanket, began fussing. Jennifer looked over at her son—saw that he had messed his pampers. She reached over and picked up the bag she had brought with her and efficiently exchanged the smelly pampers for a new pair. Then, giving Chucky a big kiss on his forehead, she turned back to her husband, saying: "Mother thinks we should have Chucky baptized."

"Baptized!" Jules sat upright. "There, what did I tell you? When is that woman going to mind her own business? And you wonder why we don't get along. Well, there's your answer. When is she going to stop meddling in our lives?"

"I know, but it is more than that." Jennifer picked her words carefully—trying hard not to cry. "Don't you think maybe—I mean—it seems like the right thing to do."

"The right thing to do!" Jules stood—armed and ready for combat. "That's what's wrong with all of you southerners. You can't do anything without wondering what other people are going to say. Well, I'll tell you one thing. No one is going to baptize my son!"

"But don't you think . . . ."

"No, I don't think. The whole thing is so much superstitious hogwash. Let me tell you a personal story I haven't shared with anyone. I was born Jewish. That meant eight days after I left my mother's womb I was circumcised. Lord, what a barbaric practice! What a painful way for an infant to enter the world! My parents told me later I had cried my eyes out for days. Oh, you have to be circumcised if you are Jewish. My whole life was shaped by being Jewish—Hebrew school and the Torah. What a lot of rubbish! And for what? So they can put the cultural stamp on you—tradition—tradition—Jews and their damn traditions. I have had it with the whole superstitions lot.

Prometheus Unbound! That's me! I don't what to be Jules the Jew. What is wrong with being just plain old Jules? I don't want my life to be defined by some religious tradition. I believe Sartre and the existentialists were right—existence precedes essence. I don't want my essence to be dictated by someone else. I wish to discover it for myself."

Chucky, who had been listening to his father voice, began to fuss—motioning for his mother to pick him up. Jennifer took her baby in her arms—comforting him and whispering loving words in his ear. Then, turning to her husband, tears in her eyes, said, "You know I don't know anything about Prometheus and existentialism. I don't care what other religions believe or don't believe. I simply miss not going to church on Sunday—of seeing my friends—of showing them Chucky—of feeling that I belong."

Jules knew he had gone too far—that his wife wasn't following his line of logic. He had known for a long

time that she did not have a carefully structured intellect—
the kind of mind you only acquire if you have done
graduate work in some intellectual discipline. He knew also
he had not wanted a Ph.D. wife. He had dated too many of
them at the university. They were stuck in their heads and
couldn't get into their bodies—all brains and no passions.
He wanted the kind of woman he had picked—someone
who was warm and real—who possessed beauty in form
and spirit. Jennifer had passed the test. What she lacked in
rationality she more than made up for in love.

Looking affectionately down at his wife and baby
son, Jules smiled and asked, "So you'd like to go to church
on Sunday? I'll tell you what we might try. Have you ever
heard about the Unitarians?"

Jennifer shook her head—still upset by Jules' harsh
words.

"There is a small gathering of Unitarians in Chapel Hill—mainly university people. We might try attending one of their services sometime. See what we think."

"What do Unitarians believe?"

Jules laughed, "That is the beauty of it. They don't have any set doctrine or creed. You can believe whatever you like. It is what I would call a thinking man's religion." Jules smiled, added, "A Unitarian is someone who has lost his gods but not his habit of going to church on Sunday."

....

It was a fine old house. The kind that was typical of the Ante-bellum South—massive front porch shaded by an ancient oak tree—thick wood moldings around the windows and doors. The original structure had been built out of rough-sawed pine. Later, a brick extension had been added. It was a house steeped in history—weathering the storms of both the Revolutionary and Civil Wars. The house had been in the Godfrey family for six generations.

Jules parked the light blue Volkswagen in the circular drive. He, Jennifer, and Chucky all got out of the car and started up the walk leading to the house. When they arrived at the top of the steps, the door to the old house was opened to greet them.

"Well, as I live and breathe." The words were those of an elderly Black woman who had exited the house to greet them. "Girl, I haven't seen you for the longest time."

"Addie," Jennifer began, "I don't think you have met my husband, Jules."

"Pleased to make your acquaintance," Addie said, extending her hand to Jules. Then, turning her attention to Chucky, she added, "And who might this be?"

"He's Chucky," Jennifer replied—holding out the baby for Addie to have a better look.

Chucky smiled—reaching out for the elderly woman.

Addie took the baby from his mother and gave him a warm hug. "He's a friendly little guy, isn't he?"

"Tell you why we dropped by," Jennifer began. "Jules is writing a paper on the history of superstition—part of his graduate studies at Duke." Jennifer flashed a look at Jules—making sure she had said the right thing. "Daddy said there were some old letters in the attic dating back to colonial times. The letters had something to do with a witch. Daddy thought Jules might find them to be of interest."

"Superstitions, witches." Addie shook her head—returning Chucky to his mother. "I don't know. I don't know anything about any old letters. We've got plenty of superstition around here already. You don't have to go looking for any witches."

49

"Jules is thinking about adding something about the Devil's Tramping Ground into his paper. You know—the place just down the road. Everyone says it's haunted. Jules thinks there might be something of interest in the old letters in the attic."

"The Devil's Tramping Ground," Addie said, shaking her head. "I don't know anything about the Devil's Tramping Ground. I don't know anything about any old letters, but you are welcome to come in and rummage through the attic. I hope you don't mind a little dust. No one has been up those stairs in years."

They all entered the house and Jennifer pointed in the direction of the staircase leading to the attic. "We'll try not to make a mess"

"Oh, don't worry about that. A little dirt never paid this old house no never mind." Then, looking at Jules, she asked, "What do you want with the Devil's Tramping Ground?"

"I'm interested in looking at it as an example of superstitions in North Carolina."

"Superstitions, I don't place much stock in fooling around with superstitions. Some things are better left alone."

Jules smiled warmly, replied, "I hope to show there isn't any Devil lurking around the Tramping Grounds."

"No Devil!" Addie's eyes open wide. "Then how do you explain all of those strange goings-on folk talk about?"

"What kind of things?" Jules asked.

"Lights, noises, they say you can't get a bird dog to go anywhere near the place."

"I suspect the lights and noises are probably just kids poking around."

Addie shook her head, turned and walked away, muttering as she went. "Superstition. No Devil. Black folk got enough to worry about without fooling around with no Devil."

Chucky reached out after Addie—as if he were trying to catch hold of her and draw her back.

Jennifer smiled, whispering to Jules, "I told you she was a little strange."

The three Steins moved through the living room and up the flight of stairs leading to the attic, which was dark and musty with only a sliver of light coming from the window at the far end of the room.

"I think Daddy said the trunk was over in the corner," Jennifer said, pointing toward a pile of dust covered boxes.

Jules began sorting through the boxes. Several were filled with old clothes—Lord only knew from which century. One had empty wine bottles. Pieces of a McClellan saddle were stuffed into a burlap sack. Some antique clocks. Finally he came to a heavy wooden trunk with metal straps. "This must be it," he announced.

Jennifer and Chucky came closer to have a look.

Jules opened the lid of the trunk—sending up a spray of fine dust. He began methodically working his way down through its contents. There was a cigar box filled with old bills and receipts; a steel bit for a horse, and some brightly colored rosettes for a bridle; a rusty pistol with no trigger; some empty shotgun shells; a family album; but no letters.

"Here, let me see what I can find," Jennifer said—handing Chucky to his father.

Jennifer took the album and seated herself on one of the boxes filled with old clothes. She began thumbing through the pages of old photographs. "Oh, look, here's a picture of Daddy when he was a little boy." She held up a black and white snapshot. "Look at his smile. Don't you think he looks just like Chucky?"

Jules glanced at the photo, nodded, continuing his digging in the trunk. Presently he came to a large, well-worn Bible. He lifted it from its place in the trunk and carried it to the window. Opening its cover sent tiny particles of dust dancing on the rays from the afternoon sun. A name was etched inside the Bible, Andrew Godfrey. A piece of crisp, yellow paper extended from the pages of the Bible. It was a handwritten letter.

"Did you find something?" Jennifer asked, setting down the album and carrying Chucky to where his father was standing.

"I think so. Listen to this." Jules began to read from the letter.

My Dear Brother Andrew,

I hope this letter finds you and your family in good spirits. I am recovering nicely from my wound. You asked me if I would risk my life for my country. Yes, I most certainly would. The victory we achieved at Moore's Creek Bridge was worth every drop of patriotic blood. We routed MacDonald and his Scottish

Loyalists. They went running for their lives.

Even you, my dear brother, must now admit

that our cause is the Will of God.

You wrote to me about the baby. Nasty business

with the witch. Of course you couldn't have

that kind of thing going on around your church.

Write soon,

Howard Godfrey

Jules searched through the Bible and the trunk

hoping to find another letter or two. No such luck. One

letter, one witch, one baby. Whatever happened to the

baby?

....

It was a hot muggy day. The red clay soil of the

piedmont was cracked and dry. North Carolina had been

without rain for weeks. After a cold and damp spring, the

weather had suddenly turned hot and dry. The tobacco plants, normally crisp and green, had started to wilt and turn a yellowish-brown. There was talk of restricting water usage in Durham and Chapel Hill.

Jules parked the light blue Volkswagen on the side the country road. He, Jennifer, and Chucky got out of the car and started up a dirt trail wandering through the woods. Pine branches extended overhead creating a canopy shutting out the rays of the afternoon sun. Halfway up the trail they came to a boggy strip of land—murky water oozing up from the bowls of the earth. Several rotten logs had been thrown into the sticky mud. Jules took Chucky and helped Jennifer across the slippery logs. Once across the bog, they continued to pick their way up the trail, coming presently to a small clearing.

"Is that it?" Jules asked, looking at the barren spot of ground in the woods.

"I guess so," Jennifer replied, "I haven't been here since I was a girl. Daddy used to go hunting out here."

Jules' face registered a look of disappointment. He had expected something more—something more than this—just a simple clearing in the woods. Surely the Devil would have picked a more impressive spot than this in order to hold dominion over the earth. "Are you sure?" he asked again.

"Yes, look at all of the empty beer cans scattered around. People come here all the time hoping to see the Devil."

"Superstitious nonsense," Jules muttered, shifting Chucky to his other arm.

"See, there is the circle where the Devil is supposed to walk?" She pointed to the worn path on the outer rim of the circle.

Jules looked carefully, said, "I don't see any difference. Dirt is just dirt." Looking at the woods around him, he asked, "Why aren't there any trees or bushes growing inside the circle?"

"No one knows."

"Here, take Chucky, I want to get a shovel from the car—dig up some soil samples to take home."

As Jules disappeared back down the trail, Jennifer discovered she and Chucky were all alone in the pine forest. Suddenly the whole world was deathly silent. Where were all the forest animals who were usually scurrying about? What had happened to the afternoon sun? A strange coolness came creeping through the trees. The silence was broken by a strange scraping sound. Jennifer looked toward two nearby pines whose branches were entangled. Odd, she thought, why hadn't she noticed them before? They were all twisted and bent out of shape—not like all the other trees that were standing only a short distance away. Her eyes drifted to the ground where some of the trees' roots were humped and knurled as if trying to escape from some

terrible pain. Jennifer suddenly felt very uncomfortable.
She moved outside the circle to where a hollow oak tree
was standing. She remembered playing around it as a girl.
She had hidden things, secret things, inside the tree. She
wondered if any of her childish treasures were still there.
Shifting Chucky to her other hip, she peered inside
the dark hole. It was empty except for a bug or two that
went scurrying back into the dark corners. Then something
caught her eye. Strange, she hadn't noticed it before. A
rusty old six cornered nail was sticking through the rotting
wood. Who had pounded it into the tree? It must have been
placed there long ago when the tree was just a sapling.

Jennifer left the tree and began walking back across
the circle. Part way across the circle something happened.
Not and event but a feeling. Standing there in the middle of
the circle she experienced the feeling of some long
forgotten memory. Dark shadows came rushing toward

her—running—running—of being chased—of falling—of spinning—twisting—turning.

Chucky suddenly began to cry, squirming in her arms as if trying to get away from some unseen evil. Jennifer left the clearing and hurried back down the path. She passed Jules on the way—returning with his shovel.

"What's the matter with Chucky? Why is he crying?"

"I don't know. Something frightened him. We'll wait for you in the car."

"Do you want me to help you across the bog?"

"No, we can manage—just don't take long. We're ready to go home."

Jules returned to the circle and dug up a sample of the hard-yellowish soil—placing in a bucket he had brought for that purpose. He smelled the dirt. It had a musty odor. Collecting his shovel and bucket, he returned to the car to discover Chucky was still crying. He cried all the way home.

. . . .

She was waiting for him at the apartment door when he arrived. "Oh, Jules, I'm so glad your home." Jennifer threw her arms around her husband's neck, giving him a desperate kiss.

"What's the matter?" He asked, as soon as he was able to untangle himself from his wife's embrace. "Has something happened to Chucky?"

Jennifer did not answer his question. Instead she pressed herself all the tighter into the security of his arms.

"What's the matter?" he asked again, giving his wife a concerned look. "I got your text message at the library. Has something happened to Chucky? I tried to call, but your phone was busy. What's wrong?"

Jennifer lifted her face from his chest—a questioning look in her eyes. Then, in the voice of a little girl, she asked, "Jules, do you love me?"

Jules looked surprised, perturbed. "Love you? Of course I love you. What has that got to do with anything?"

Jennifer kissed him passionately.

"Why did you call—leave a message—say that it was important? I was in the middle of doing my research."

"Jules," she began, a distant look in her eyes, "do you think I'm normal? I mean, do you think I'm crazy, do you?"

"Crazy, of course not!" and he added teasingly, "A little neurotic maybe, but hell, all women are that way. Freud once said he had answered all the big questions in psychoanalysis except one: What does a woman want?"

Jennifer's expression changed to one of hurt. "You didn't have to say that."

Oh, all right, I'm sorry, but why did you call?"

"Well, I was looking through the old family album, you know, the one we brought home from the attic."

"Okay."

"There were some old photographs dating back to the time of the Civil War. I was looking through them when I came across a couple of old letters."

"Letters," Jules was suddenly interested, "Did you find the other pages to the Reverend's letter?"

"No, but there were some letters about my great, great, grandfather. I called mother to see what she knew about him. That's probably why my phone was busy."

"Where are the letters?" Jules asked, becoming increasing impatient with his wife's drawn out storytelling.

"There're on the kitchen table."

Jules hurried into the kitchen. He was followed closely by his wife. The table was covered with old photographs. Jennifer picked one and handed it to her husband. The picture was of a gray-bearded man with deep set eyes.

"This picture is of great, great, grandfather, Clarence Godfrey. Mother says he fought in the Civil War. He lost a leg at the battle of Stone Mountain. Those letters were written by his wife, Nancy, to her sister Margaret, but they were apparently never mailed. Maybe because the war interrupted the mail service, I don't know." Jennifer pointed to several yellow-stained letters lying on the table. "They say when he returned home from the war the Yankees and Carpetbaggers had stolen most of his land. He couldn't work the land because he only had one leg. He carved himself a wooden leg out of an old tree stump, but he couldn't wear it very long because it rubbed against the bone in his leg. When they cut off his leg, they didn't treat the nerves properly. He suffered a lot of pain. I guess that is why he drank so much."

"Surgical techniques were pretty primitive back then. That is why they used to call surgeons saw-bones. As many men died on the operating table as were killed on the battlefield."

Jennifer picked up some other old papers and handed them to her husband. "These, I think, were cut or pulled out of a diary."

"What makes you think that?"

"Because when I was a girl, I kept a diary. When I was angry with people—Mom and Dad—I would write nasty things about them in my diary. Later, when I realized how hurtful my words were, I would pull out those pages and throw them in my secret box for storing nasty notes."

"Weren't you a naughty little girl," Jules said in a teasing manner.

Jennifer flushed, embarrassed. "The pages say one evening Granddaddy put on his wooden leg, saddled his horse, and rode into town. While he was there, he drank more than he should have."

Jules looked at the picture and the crumpled yellow pages. "Yeah, he looks like the kind of guy who could really stow it away."

"No, Jules, listen, this is sad. On his way home from town the horse was frightened by something. Granddaddy was thrown—knocked unconscious. When he came around, he was face-to-face with the Devil."

"The Devil!"

"Yes, the Devil had granddaddy by his wooden leg and was trying to pull him down a dark hole. Granddaddy hollered, beat the Devil off with his pistol."

Jules laughed openly, "Lord, he must have really been stoned."

"When granddaddy didn't come home, they went out looking for him. They found him the next day hobbling around in the woods, dazed and confused. He had lost his wooden leg, and he kept mumbling the story about the Devil. Later, they found the horse and his pistol, but they never found his wooden leg. Do you think the pistol could be the same one we saw in the trunk?"

"Probably," Jules said, looking intently at his wife, "but what has all of that got to do with why you called me, left a message?"

A distant look returned to Jennifer's eyes. "Granddaddy never recovered from the experience. They say he went to bed and only sat up to eat and use the bedpan. He muttered all the time about the Devil trying to drag him down a dark hole. He seems to have lost his mind. Isn't that sad?"

"Yes, I guess so, but what does all of that have to do with why you called?'

Jennifer looked intently into her husband's eyes, asked, "Jules, do you think insanity runs in families?"

Jules burst into laughter. "Lord, of course not. That idea went out with witchcraft!"

"Why do you think granddaddy lost his mind?"

"Probably because he drank too much. Mental wards are filled with alcoholics."

"What about the Devil? Do you think granddaddy really saw the Devil?

"Only in the windmills of his mind."

....

Jennifer's back was turned toward him when he entered the room. She was folding clothes, stacking them on the bed. She was dressed in a pair of faded blue Levi's and one of his old sweatshirts. Her light brown hair was pinned casually on top of her head. Jules liked her just that way, raw sexuality. The Levi's accentuated the curve of her tight little ass. He liked women with round, firm asses. A pretty ass trumped everything. Some guys were big on tits—the bigger the better. Others went ecstatic about hair, eyes, and lips. Those things were okay, but they only added to the package. A pretty ass, however, that was something to write home about.

The first time he had laid eyes on Jennifer was when she was walking across campus. Impulsively, his gaze drifted to the sway of her ass. He had decided right then and there, on the walk leading to the library, he had to meet that woman. Screwing up his courage and putting on his best manners, Jules had introduced himself. And the rest was history. Stepping up behind his wife, Jules ran his hand over her lovely ass.

"Oh, Jules," Jennifer turned, startled. "I didn't hear you come in." She glanced at the clock on the dresser, asked, "What are you doing home so early?"

Jules wrapped his arms around her waist—kissing her passionately on the neck. "I'll give you one guess."

Jennifer flushed. "Oh, Jules, no, not now! I've got to finish folding the clothes, and I haven't started dinner."

"Screw dinner," he said, pulling her down on the bed and knocking the stack of towels on the floor.

"Jules no, I need to take a shower, and . . . ."

Jennifer's words were cut short by the force of his mouth over hers. Her Levi's quickly took their place on the floor next to the towels. Jennifer's protests were cut short by the passion of her husband's embrace.

Jules looked down at his wife, commenting with approval: "You still have a pretty nice body for a woman who recently gave birth to a nine pound baby boy."

Jennifer's eyes darted upward, questioning, "What's that supposed to mean?"

"Oh, you know, for just having given birth, you don't show too many signs of wear and tear."

Jennifer moved to the other side of the bed, turning her back toward her husband.

"What's the matter?" Jules asked, puzzled. "I was just trying to pay you a compliment."

"Well, if that's the best you can do, you can keep your compliments to yourself."

Jules moved closer to his wife, kissing her lightly on the neck. "Guess what I was reading today?"

Jennifer said nothing.

"I was reading about witchcraft." Jules rolled his wife over to face him—lifting her sweatshirt to expose her breasts. "And you know what? You have the mark of a witch."

"No I don't!" Jennifer replied in a huff, pulling down her sweatshirt.

"No, don't get mad—here I'll show you." Lifting her sweatshirt once more, he pointed to the bluish mole just under her left breast. "There, you see, it's a third tit—the mark of a witch."

Jennifer looked, replied, "That's nothing. I've had that all my life."

"Remember when you were nursing Chucky, how it puffed up."

"Yes, but it has gone down now."

"They say that is the mark of a witch."

"Oh, Jules, you make me so mad. If all you came home for was to make fun of me . . . ."

Jules caught hold of his wife—kissing her passionately—preventing her from leaving the bed. "Don't get all up tight. I'm just trying to tell you what I was reading, witchcraft."

Jennifer was not pacified.

Jules kissed her again, adding, "Seriously, a witch is supposed to have a mark just like yours."

"Well, I'm not a witch!"

"I know, but if you had lived back in Colonial New England, they might have mistaken you for a witch."

"How could anyone possibly know that I have a mole under my breast?"

"Easy, if you were suspected of practicing witchcraft, they would bring you before a jury of women and have you examined. If they saw the mark, they would declare you to be a witch."

"Oh, Jules, I've never heard of such a thing. I think you're just making this up in order to tease me."

"No, it all came out during the Salem Witch Trials."

"I have always thought the Pilgrims were such religious people."

"Religious! Lord, who do you suppose conducted the witch trials? The clergy—Cotton Mather and his faithful flock—were the witch hunters."

"I think that is awful—just because someone has a mole in the wrong place."

"Listen, if they couldn't find the mark on you, they would bind your right thumb to your left big toe, and your left thumb to your right one, and throw you in one of New England's famous ponds. If you didn't drown, they would know you were a witch."

"What if I drown?"

"Then they would know you were not a witch."

"But I would be dead."

"Yes, but you would be free of the charge of witchcraft."

"Well, if they threw me into a pond, they would have to find me not guilty because I can't swim."

Jules laughed, adding, "There are records of old women who were thought be witches who were thrown overboard at sea."

"That's just awful. Why would they do such a thing?"

"If the ship were caught in a big storm, they would blame the storm on the witch. What was the answer? Toss the old woman overboard."

"I'm glad I didn't live back then."

"If you had, they would have found you guilty of witchcraft, and witches were suspected of making love to the Devil." A strange, funny smile crept across Jules' face.

"What's the matter?" Jennifer asked, giving her husband a questioning look.

Jules laughed a strange, loud, demonic laugh. "I'm the Devil and I've come to take possession of your body."

"Oh, Jules, don't!" Jennifer struggled to free herself from his grip. "You'll give me bad dreams."

. . . .

There was a loud crash. Jules sat upright in bed. He glanced at the clock on the dresser, five o'clock.

"What's the matter? Jennifer asked, peering over at her husband.

"I heard something—a loud noise from the kitchen."

"I didn't hear anything."

"That's because you sleep like a horse," Jules said, slipping his legs out of bed and looking for his robe.

"Are you getting up?"

"What does it look like?"

"Do you want me to come with you?"

"Suit yourself."

"Please be careful."

Jules left the bedroom and walked quietly down the hallway leading to the kitchen. As he entered the kitchen, something shot pass him—something small and furry. "Rotten cat!" he muttered. Flipping on the light, he swore again. "Damn!" Jennifer's planter box, which had been located in the window, was lying on the floor. Dirt and bean sprouts where scattered in all directions. "Damn!" he said once more.

"What's the matter," Jennifer asked, appearing at the kitchen door.

"Oh, the damn cat tipped over the planter box where I was trying to grow some beans in the soil I brought home from inside the circle at Devil's Tramping Ground. God, what a mess!"

"Can you save any of them?"

"No, they are all smashed to hell!"

"It's just as well. They weren't growing anyway— shriveled leaves and yellow stems. I'll be glad to have them out of the kitchen."

Jules flashed his wife a perturbed look. "That's just the point. I wanted to see if anything could grow in that soil."

"Well, it seems to me you have already shown that. They were such pathetic little plants."

"Yeah—but—okay—go ahead and throw it all away."

Just then the cat returned to the kitchen—humped its back—hissed—jumped up on the counter—then back to the floor—dashed wildly around the kitchen.

"What's the matter with the cat?" Jennifer asked.

"How should I know? The crazy damn cat needs to go outside."

Jules caught the cat and took her to the front door—tossing her out into the night. When he returned to the kitchen, Jennifer was busy cleaning up the mess on the floor.

"Why don't you go back to bed," she said wearily.

That is exactly what he did while Jennifer finished sweeping and mopping the floor. In the morning they looked for the cat. It was nowhere to be found.

....

It was a bright sunny day—just the kind of day for a picnic. Jennifer had packed the picnic basket, and Jules had stopped by Colonel Sanders and picked up a bucket of Kentucky Fried Chicken. They had agreed to meet Jennifer's parents at Durham's Life and Science Museum. Everything had gone off like clockwork. Before sitting down for lunch, Jennifer's mother had suggested a short walk would be nice. Her father, on the other hand, had volunteered to say behind and guard the picnic basket.

Grace, Jennifer, Chucky, and Jules all started up the nature trail leading through the woods. Along the trail were plaster representations of prehistoric reptiles. They quickly passed by the Eryops, the Dimetrodon, and the Plateosaurus. Then, crossing over a small wooden bridge, they came face to face with a large dinosaur.

"Oh, look, Chucky," Grace exclaimed, "see the dragon!"

Jules frowned, whispered to his son, "It's not a dragon. Dragons are mythical creatures. It's a Brontosaurus that lived 150 million years ago."

Chucky seemed equally unimpressed by either answer.

The party continued up the trail until they came to the cage housing the live bears. Chucky smiled and pointed at the bears. He laughed at the cub splashing in a pool of water.

"I'd like to take Chucky to see the display on evolution," Jules suggested.

"Oh, Jules," Jennifer replied, "he won't understand it."

"You don't know," Jules insisted. "There are studies on retroactive inhibition that suggest that once something is learned it is never completely forgotten. That is why I asked you to listen to classical music while Chucky was still in the womb."

"I know and I did, but I still think it is a silly idea."

"I'm going back to the table," Grace said, addressing herself to her daughter. "You can go on with Jules if you wish."

"No, I'll come with you."

With that Jules and Chucky were left alone to forage for themselves. Walking a short distance, they came to the building housing the display on evolution. Jules began rattling off the facts about Dr. Leakey—the significance of his finds in East Africa—the subtle points about Zinjanthropus—the development of Cro-magnon Man, and the hoax surrounding Piltdown Man. While his father was engaged in explaining all of the twists and turns in human evolution, Chucky sucked on his thumb and watched a group of Brownie Scouts who were passing by.

Having finished with the museum, Jules and Chucky worked their way back down the trail to the picnic table. Jules handed Chucky off to his mother, and began filling his paper plate with chicken, potato salad, and coleslaw.

"Tasty chicken," Charles said, having filled his plate as well.

"Yes," Jennifer agreed, "but the price has really gone up. I can remember when we only had to pay half as much for the same meal."

"It's that way with everything," Grace confirmed. "The government ought to do something about it."

"The stock market has dropped again," Charles observed. "It has dropped five hundred points in the last month—reflecting the unhealthy mood of the country."

"Someone ought to do something about government spending," Grace remarked. "Look at all the money they've thrown away on family support programs. It's the reason you can't hire any decent help."

"Bull!" Jules said, struggling not to cough up his chicken. "If you want to know the reason for inflation, look no farther than the big corporations. Look at what they have done to the price of gas in the last month. There isn't such a thing as a free market anymore. All of the prices are administered by the big corporations."

"Well, I think Washington should do something," Grace insisted.

"Washington isn't going to do anything," Jules asserted. "They've all sold their souls to the billionaire's club. Look at the free rein they have given Jeff Bazos and Amazon. He hasn't paid a penny in income tax for years. The same is true of all the billionaire leaches."

"Maybe if we were to elect a good southern conservative to the White House," Charles said, taking another chicken wing. "That just might be what the country needs."

Jules coughed, looking like he was trying to force down an explosion of distasteful words.

Jennifer handed Chucky a chicken leg from which she had already stripped most of the meat.

"I don't think he should have that," Grace said, giving her daughter a disapproving look.

"I'm sure it won't hurt him. He eats things like this all the time."

"He'll get it all over his new clothes."

"Oh, well, they need to be washed anyway."

Chucky sucked on the bone, obviously enjoying the flavor of the chicken.

Several Yellow Jackets had been hovering over the table—attracted by the smell of the chicken. Jules swished them away with the lid that came with the bucket of chicken.

"You don't have to worry about them," Charles said. "They're what we call sweat bees. They won't sting you as long as you leave them alone."

"I've never liked bees," Jennifer said. "Remember when I knocked down a bee hive with a long stick, and they chased me into the house."

"Do you still remember that?" Grace replied. "We were out at the old house. I thought you were playing skip-rope, but here you came running into the house with the bees in hot pursuit. What made you think to knock down the bee hive?"

"I don't know. I just didn't like them."

"That's because when you were a little girl you came running home one day crying. A big Bumble Bee had gotten tangled up in your hair and couldn't get free. I think you were more frightened than hurt."

"Mother," Jennifer looked embarrassed. "Don't tell that story anymore."

"Why, not—it's true—isn't it Charles?"

"Who did you see at church?" Jennifer asked, hoping to change the topic of conversation.

"Oh, dear, you should have been there. Everyone asked about you. Mary Ellen—you remember her—she married the Mitchell boy—who went to your old high school. She just returned from a vacation in Hawaii—had the most wonderful tan. They're going to have their baby baptized next Sunday. Why don't you plan on attending? I'm sure they would be happy to see you."

Chucky suddenly gave out a sharp cry. All eyes turned in his direction. A large Yellow Jacket had settled on his hand holding the chicken bone. It was in the process of slowly, methodically lowering its stinger into his thumb.

Jennifer sprang into action—swatting the bee and the chicken bone across the table. All of the instincts of motherhood registered on her face.

Chucky began crying loudly.

"You should try to get some ice on his thumb," Charles suggested.

"We should first try to get the stinger out," Jules offered.

"I remember when you were a little girl," Grace began.

"We'll wait for all of you in the car," Jennifer replied, standing and clutching her baby tightly against her breasts.

…………..

Running—panic—terror—a pounding heart—air—gasping for air—swirling clouds of darkness—fleeting shadows—distorted images—mocking faces—dogs barking—running—falling—swirling—blackness.

"No!" Jennifer screamed, sitting upright in bed.

"What's the matter?" Jules asked, more asleep then awake.

"My dream, I had that awful dream again."

"Oh, is that all."

"Is that all? You wouldn't say that if it were your dream."

"Okay, tell me about it so we can go back to sleep."

"No, not if that's the way you are going to look at it."

Jules reached over and pulled his wife down next to him. "Okay, tell me about your bad dream. I want to hear it."

Jennifer waited several minutes before beginning. "Well, it is like people are chasing me. I don't know who they are. I didn't see any faces. I have had the same dream many times in my life." She moved closer to her husband "It's always the same. I'm running, trying to get away. Then I trip and fall. That's when I wake up."

Jules kissed his wife on the forehead. "Are you being chased by men?"

"I think so, but I never get to see their faces."

"When you're having your dream, do you ever see knives, pitchforks, or guns?"

"Sometimes."

"Do you run across rolling hills covered with flowers."

"How did you know?"

"And at the end of the dream do you start falling?"

"That's exactly how I feel."

"And you've had this dream many times?"

"As long as I can remember."

"Do you want to know what Freud would say about your dream?"

"Freud?" Jennifer gave her husband a puzzled look.

Jules laughed openly. "He'd say you were sexually frustrated."

"Oh, Jules!" Jennifer pulled away from her husband.

Jules laughed openly, adding: "No, really, dreams are wishful filling. Your Id was having a sexual holiday while your Super-Ego was away on vacation."

"Oh, I don't believe that."

"It's true. Read any book on psychoanalysis."

There was a small cry from the other bedroom.

"What's the matter with Chucky?' Jules whispered.

"I don't know. He's probably wet—needs to be changed."

They lay quietly for several minutes. There were no more noises from the other bedroom.

Jennifer was the first to break the silence. "Jules?"

"Yes."

"I'd like to take Chucky to see the pediatrician. He hasn't been feeling well—not wanting to eat his meals."

"Do you have to take him this month?"

"I would like to. Why?"

"It's just that the checking account is dry. My scholarship money hasn't been deposited. But if you think he needs to see the pediatrician, well, go ahead and take him. We'll find the money someplace."

Another silence followed.

"Jules?"

"Yes."

"What do you suppose happened to the cat?"

"Who knows—probably got run over."

"Oh, I hope not."

"Well, whatever happened, it's gone. I've looked up and down the block a dozen times. No cat!"

"Do you think we could have another cat? I know Chucky would like to have one."

"Why don't we wait until we have a place of our own. It's hard to keep a pet in an apartment. Maybe we could get a dog. Every boy should have a dog."

"That would be nice."

Jennifer snuggled closer to her husband. She liked the feel of his warm, protective arms around her. She lay very still—hardly daring to breath. Presently Jules began to snore. She closed her eyes—tried to drift back to sleep. But it was no use. She was still upset about her dream. Maybe Jules and Freud were right—just a sexual fantasy. No, her feelings told her there was more to it than that. What about—she hated to even think about it—didn't dare to tell Jules because of what he might say—make fun of her—no, she would put it out of her mind—try to go back to sleep. But try as she might, Jennifer did not sleep anymore that night.

. . . .

Chucky Stein was crying. He had started crying the minute his mother had removed his pamper. He knew where he was—what to expect—and no amount of soft talk from his mother was going to convince him otherwise. The chilly, narrow little room with its shiny white walls—the smell of alcohol and disinfectant—all told him the same story. Watch out Chucky! The doctor is coming!

The nurse entered the room and took his temperature, which she recorded on a chart. Before leaving the room, she said in a reassuring voice, "The doctor will be with you shortly."

Jennifer picked up her baby and tried to comfort him. She showed him the brightly colored drawings on the wall—Jack and Jill going up the hill—but Chucky could not be pacified.

"Well, who have we here?" The question came from Doctor Davis, who was an elderly man with silver-gray hair.

Chucky took one look at the doctor and cried all the louder.

"How has he been?" Doctor Davis asked, looking at Jennifer.

"He hasn't been feeling well. He wakes up at night, and he hasn't been eating like he should." Prying herself free from Chucky's grip, she handed her baby to Doctor Davis.

Chucky screamed loudly, reaching out for his mother.

Doctor Davis laid Chucky on a table, saying reassuringly, "There, there, little fellow, we're not going to hurt you."

Chucky screamed all the louder.

The doctor placed his stethoscope on Chucky's chest and listened carefully to his heart beat. Then he turned Chucky over and listened to his breathing. Finally, looking over at Jennifer, he remarked, "Well, there is nothing wrong with his lungs."

Jennifer flashed the doctor a polite smile. She wished he would hurry with the examination. She wanted to hold and comfort her baby.

Doctor Davis picked up his otoscope and looked into Chucky's ears. The tongue depressor came next. Chucky gagged.

Jennifer felt faint.

Doctor Davis flashed a pen light into Chucky's eyes. He felt his neck and abdomen for signs of distension. Turning to Jennifer, he asked, "Has he been vomiting?"

"No," Jennifer replied.

Doctor Davis picked up Chucky's chart and scribbled a few lines. Looking at Jennifer, he said, "You can go ahead and get him dressed." With that the doctor left the room.

Jennifer replaced Chucky's pampers. She also slipped on his shirt and pants. Finally, she picked up her crying baby and tried to comfort him.

Finally, Doctor Davis returned and said, "Chucky has had his DPT, and he won't need his shot for measles for two more months. As far as his general health is concerned, his temperature is normal and his heart and lungs sound good." Glancing down at Chucky's chart, he added, "You were right about his appetite. He hasn't been gaining weight the way he was before. But it is nothing to become alarmed about. Children often go through cycles of eating. Sometimes they eat; sometimes they don't. You say he is restless at night?"

"Yes, he cries in his sleep."

"That might be because he is teething. Has he shown any signs of a rash?"

"No, not that I'm aware of."

Doctor Davis lifted Chucky's shirt.

Chucky pulled away, clinging to his mother.

"When I was examining Chucky, I noticed he has a birthmark on his chest." The doctor pointed to a bluish-black mark on Chucky's chest. "We don't have a record of it on his chart. Is it something he has developed recently?"

Jennifer looked worried. "No, I don't think so. I don't remember the first time I noticed it."

"Well, we must have overlooked it on your earlier visits. It's nothing to worry about, not unless it starts to grow." Lowering Chucky's shirt, he added, "Chucky seems to be more nervous than usual. Have there been any changes at home?"

Jennifer looked puzzled, asked, "Changes?"

"Yes, how is your relationship with your husband? Are you getting a divorce?"

"Divorce, oh, heavens no!"

Doctor Davis smiled. "I always ask that question when a baby seems emotional and upset. Children often reflect the emotional climate of what is going on at home. A nervous baby can mean a tense mother."

"Well, there isn't going to be a divorce," Jennifer said flatly.

Doctor Davis nodded his head, replied, "See my assistant on your way out. Make an appointment for two months from now. Be sure and call if anything changes in Churcky's life." Having said his piece, the doctor left the room.

Jennifer finished gathering up her things, purse and bag. She knew she should feel better, reassured. After all Doctor Davis was one of the best pediatricians in the city. She ought to be willing to accept his word that nothing was seriously wrong with Chucky. But somehow she knew there was something missing—something that had gone unsaid. She worried about the bluish mole on Chucky's chest. When had she first noticed it? Had it been there when she had taken him home from the hospital? She wanted to tell Jules, but he might laugh and say that now there was not only a witch but also a warlock in the family.

No, she couldn't tell Jules. He wouldn't understand. It would have to remain her secret—at least for now.

....

Jules left the library and hurried down the sidewalk. He had an anxious knot in the pit of his stomach. Why in the world had she called—left him a text message—wanted to meet him at Duke's Cathedral? What had gone wrong? Why was she at the Cathedral?

Jules turned the corner and came into full view of Duke's Gothic Cathedral. Years ago he had read a history written by Crane Brinton, who described the aesthetics of medieval architecture. Jules had always marveled at its architecture, massive yet delicate. Not like a Greek temple. Greek temples sat four-square, tied to the earth. Their basic shape was no more inspiring than a box. Gothic cathedrals, on the other hand, tried to ascend the boundaries of space and time. Through the use of such imaginative inventions as the pointed arch and the flying buttress, medieval craftsmen had translated into stone a sense of wonder and awe. The Greek temple was geometry; the Gothic cathedral was algebra. The Greek temple accepted man's limitations. The Gothic cathedral aspired to transcend them. The Greek temple looked like it had been constructed by human hands. The Gothic cathedral looked like it had been grown by the forest.

Jules opened one of the heavy oak doors and entered the twilight of the Cathedral. He found Jennifer seated on one of the back rows. She did not move to greet him when he joined her on the bench. Her tear-stained face was fixed on the altar at the front of the hall.

"What's the matter, honey?" Jules asked, placing his arm around his wife's shoulder. "Where's Chucky? Has something happened?"

Jennifer turned to face her husband, a lost look in her eyes.

Jules repeated his question. "Where's Chucky? Is he all right?"

Jennifer's reply came from a hushed voice—as if she were a long way off. "Chucky, oh, he's fine—at home asleep."

"You left him alone?" Jules asked, clearly puzzled. It wasn't like Jennifer to leave Chucky alone.

"He's all right. I finally got him to sleep—thought I'd take a walk." There was a distant, broken quality in her voice. "I'm sorry if I interrupted your studies, but I couldn't help myself."

Jules looked at his wife. He had never seen her like this before. He had an uneasy feeling about this whole conversation.

"I don't know why I stopped here," Jennifer began. "I knew I should go home and check on Chucky, but I couldn't. I just couldn't!" Jennifer began to cry once more.

Jules put his arm around his wife's shoulder, pulling her closer to him, saying: "Come on, I'll take you home. You're probably just tired."

"No," she exclaimed, showing a sudden burst of anger. "That's not it! I'm not tired! It's . . . ." Her voice trailed off into a gush of tears.

"Don't cry," Jules whispered softly, glancing around the room to see if anyone was listening. "Have I done something to upset you?"

"No, it's nothing you've done. It's just . . . ." More tears.

Jules removed a handkerchief from his pocket and handed it to his wife. Jennifer dabbed at her mascara-stained eyes.

After a long pause, Jules finally asked, "Are you feeling any better?"

Jennifer nodded.

"Do you think you can tell me what's wrong?"

Jennifer nodded, began: "This afternoon I started thinking how things were when I was a little girl. I always felt loved. My Daddy always used to hold me on his lap and tell me I was the joy in his life. I always felt warm and protected."

"Well, you're my little girl now," Jules said, affectionately slipping his hand into his wife's and pressing her fingers tightly. "I thought you knew that."

Jennifer smiled slightly, continued: "After I said my prayers, my parents always came up to my room and tucked me into bed. I always asked God to look after all of the members of my family—not to let anything bad happen to anyone. I used to believe if I didn't say my prayers something awful would happen."

Jules smiled, kissing his wife on the cheek. "That's was just a little girl's way of looking at the world."

"I know, but that's how I felt. And that feeling—the way I used to feel when I had forgotten to say my prayers—well, that's how I felt this evening. That's why I stopped here—why I called you."

"You silly little girl. Nothing bad is going to happen to any of us. The world doesn't run on childish prayers."

"I know," Jennifer confessed, looking embarrassed. "But it always made me feel better."

"Well, I love you, and I always will."

"I know," Jennifer said, turning and looking at the stained-glass windows at the far end of the cathedral. The light from the afternoon sun created a brilliant mosaic of reds, greens, and blues. "Jules?" she asked.

"Yes."

"Do you believe birds are messengers from heaven? The other day a Hummingbird came right up to where Chucky and I were sitting. He stopped right in front of Chucky and just stood there in midair. He looked like he was trying to tell Chucky something—a message from heaven. I think he was trying to tell Chucky something about the mole on his chest."

The secret was out!

....

Chapter 3

The University

Jules was seated at one end of a large oval table, which was located in the conference room of the History Department at Duke University. Seated around the table were the faculty members serving on his doctoral committee. Their names read like a *Who's Who* in higher education. At the other end of the table was seated Professor Peterson, who was Jules' major professor and Chairman of the Department of History. His academic specialty was American History, particularly the Civil War. Jules considered him to be a fair-minded and even temper man. Seated to Peterson's left was Professor Archer. Her research area was Modern European History. Students, when speaking in private, referred to her as the Barracuda. She had a sharp mind and an even sharper tongue; she was intolerant of sloppy thinking. To Peterson's right was seated Professor Kanumba. He had joined the faculty of the Department of African-American Studies five years earlier and had already established himself as a nationally recognized scholar. Seated at the other end of the table, closer to Jules, was Professor Cooper, who specialized in Western Intellectual History. He had recently published a book on Peter Abelard, who was a medieval scholar at the University of Paris. Directly across from Cooper was Professor Chillcott, who was an archeologist who had made a scholarly name for himself by translating Ancient Egyptian Hieroglyphics. Jules had taken course work with all of them.

Professor Peterson opened the meeting by saying, "I'm glad you could all make it. Unfortunately, that is not always the case. Faculty can find as many reasons for avoiding meetings as dogs can find for scratching at fleas. It's good to have everyone's input when it comes to evaluating a candidate's record. I trust you all know Mr. Stein, who is seated at the other end of the table. He is one of our scholars funded by the National Humanities Center. Why don't we start by having Mr. Stein tell us a little about his academic background and what brought him to Duke.

Jules' heart suddenly skipped a beat. The blood drained from his face, and his hands grew clammy. So this was how it felt when they called out—Dead Man Walking! "Well," Jules began, "my undergraduate major was in history, and I accepted a teaching position at a high school in Virginia. I am not sure how much I taught the students, but they taught me a great deal. I believe public school experience is vital if you wish to learn how to teach. The children are brutally honest. They'll tell you upfront when you are boring, and when they don't understand one of your lessons. I was at the high school for five years when I received an offer to teach at a junior college in Raleigh. I was there when I applied for and received the National Humanities Fellowship to study at Duke.

Professor Archer, who had been sitting quietly studying Jules' composure, glanced at Professor Peterson as if asking permission to open the questioning. Peterson nodded his consent. "Congratulations, Mr. Stein, you did very well on your written examinations, which I am sure everyone around this table already knows. Let's see if we can find out what it is that you don't know. You wish to become a scholar. Very well. That means research and publication. Historically, from which country did we borrow the Ph.D. degree?

Jules nodded knowingly. "If I am not mistaken, it comes from 19th century Prussia, modern Germany. They had a tradition of awarding a Ph.D. to their university graduates. Part of that tradition was the belief that a scholar should pick a theme and spend a good part of his (her) life becoming an authority on that particular subject."

"Good, Mr. Stein, I see from your course work you have taken classes all over campus, which is evident from the composition of your committee. You have a very eclectic mind. My question is this: What will you select as your research theme?"

Trapped! The Barracuda had him. How could he weasel out of this one? He hated narrow, thematic research. Learning should be mind expanding, not laced in on all sides by tradition. Damn the Prussians and their Ph.D.! How to answer her question? Finally, he replied: "I've had a long-standing interest in superstition—how it has not only shaped the world's great religions, but how it has filtered down into everyday life. I believe one of the root metaphors haunting humanity is what we might call the puppet syndrome. It is the belief that someone, gods or fate, is pulling the strings affecting human actions. The story of Job in the *Old Testament* is an excellent example. God and Satan made a wager about Job's faithfulness. Job's tests do not stop until he admits that the ways of God are unknowable by ordinary mortals."

Professor Kanumba suddenly jumped into the conversation as if launched by a springboard. "Superstition! The Black experience is rife with superstitions. All of the things Black people were supposed to be or not to be. Black history is stacked high with examples of superstitions—the doctrine of the natural slave, Jim Crow and segregation, the current efforts by the Republican Party to exclude Blacks from voting. Racism and superstition have marched hand-in-hand through the pages of American history."

"That's exactly the kind of connections," Jules said, "that I'm interested in writing about. All the way from 1619 to the insurrection at the Capitol in 2021, racism and White supremacy have been reoccurring themes in American society. Even supposedly scientific studies have been touched by racism. We have only to look at the book published by Herrnstein and Murray, *The Bell Curve,* to see how superstition parades around in the guise of statistics."

Professor Chillcott, who had been waiting patiently to join the conversation, said: "I know you are familiar with the Egyptian Pharaoh, Akhenaten."

"Yes," Jules replied, "he's the one who is usually credited with the idea of monotheism, which was later incorporated in the Hebrew faith by Moses, or so the story goes."

"Correct," Chillcott replied, "What I would like to know is do you agree or disagree with Ingersoll when he said: An honest God is the noblest work of man?"

Jules thought for a moment before responding. "An honest God is clearly preferable to an dishonest one, which was all too often the case with the Greeks and the Romans. Though the idea of an honest God was a step forward in the evolution of religious thought, I do not believe it was or should become the last. I would agree with John Dewey in his book, *A Common Faith*, that religious feelings, adjectives, can be separated from their antecedent doctrines, nouns, so that feelings of dedication to higher principles can be fused into such values as democracy and the common dignity of all mankind."

"Dewey also went on to argue," Professor Cooper interjected, "that the word God, if we wish to retain it, could be redefined to mean the active interrelationship between the ideal and the actual. How many Southern Baptists do you know who would find Dewey's definition to be an attractive alternative to Jesus Loves Me This I Know?"

All the members of the committee laughed.

"Well, Jules," Professor Peterson said, taking charge of the meeting, "why don't you explain to the committee what you have in mind for a dissertation?"

Jules nodded, relieved to be back on his own turf. "I want to show how superstition not only underlies all of the world's great religions, but how it underscores the entire fabric of social philosophy."

The faculty gathered around the table shook their heads—a couple even laughing.

Professor Cooper was the first to speak. "Son, how many years do you plan on staying here at Duke working on your dissertation?"

"Yes," Professor Archer added, "it took Toynbee a lifetime to write his study of the rise and fall of 21 different world civilizations. How long is your fellowship going to pay for your study?"

"You need to pick a topic that is manageable— something you can finish in a year or two," Professor Kanumba advised.

If you wish to do something on superstition, why don't you select something closer to home? North Carolina is rich in superstitions—all the way from the believers in the Walking Dead on the coast to the Snake Handlers of Appalachia," Professor Chillcott suggested.

"Jules, you've been telling me stories about the Devil's Tramping Ground, which is located next to some property owned by your wife's family." Professor Peterson noted. "What about digging into the state's archives and writing up a complete history of the place?"

"Yes," Professor Cooper confirmed, a touch of irony in his voice, "you might even become the world's leading authority on the Devil's Tramping Ground. That should satisfy even the most rigid apostles of Prussian style research."

All the members of the committee laughed—stood and prepared to leave—confident they had steered another doctoral student in the right direction.

....

Jules found himself standing in front of a classroom filled with undergraduate students at Duke University. Standing next to him was Professor Peterson, who was waving his hand in the air, signaling the students to quiet down so the class could begin. Professor Peterson started: "Welcome back from your summer vacation. I'm sure you're all enthusiastic to resume your university studies." There was laughing, grumbling, and a number of "Oh sure." Professor Peterson continued with his introduction. "This is History 155, Themes in the American Experience. If you are not registered for this class, this is an opportune time to leave." All the students remained seated. "Well, it looks like we are all in the right place at the right time. Let me introduce your instructor for this semester, Mr. Stein. He is one of our outstanding graduate students. We believe Mr. Stein shows good promise of becoming a published scholar. I will leave you in his tender care. Have a good semester." And with those parting words, Professor Peterson disappeared out the door.

Alone, all alone—standing in front of a classroom filled with strange and enquiring faces. What kind of a class would they prove to be? In high school the students let you know who they were right off. College students were different—standoffish—skeptical—judgmental—hard to read. What were they thinking? Well, it was now or never. The appointed hour had arrived. Jules began: "As Professor Peterson told you this is History 155, Themes in the American Experience. We have selected two textbooks for this class, Jon Meacham's *The Soul of America,* and David Rubenstein's *The American Story.* Jules went to the board and wrote down the name of the class and the required textbooks. "Now I want to pass around a seating chart." He held up a yellow manila folder. You will see that it is all laid out in terms of little squares. The trick is to find your square. Is everyone seated where he or she wishes to be for the rest of the semester?" There were glances around the room, but everyone stayed seated. "Very well. You have to look at the chart from my point of view, which is a mirror image of your point of view. I will start the chart down each row. When it comes to the end of the row, pass it forward so we can start it down the next row. Just fill in the blank square below the student who is seated in front of you." With that Jules started the chart down the row located on the left side of the classroom, noting that the student's name was Jim Baker. When the seating chart was half way down the row, Jules turned to Jim and asked: "Well, Jim, this class is about themes in American history. What do you suppose one of those themes might be?"

Jim looked like he had been suddenly ambushed. "I watched an old movie the other night, *How The West Was Won,* would that qualify as a theme?"

"Great!" Jules exclaimed. "*How The West Was Won*—an oldie but a goodie. That is clearly a theme in

American history. There was a 19th century historian by the name of Fredrick Jackson Turner. He read his dissertation, or at least part of it, at the 1893 World's Fair in Chicago. His thesis was that the frontier movement in American history had been the central experience shaping the national character we have come to think of as distinctly American. Was he right? That is one of the themes we will want to explore during the semester."

The seating chart had been returned to the front of the second row. Jules picked it up and showed the girl in the second row where to place her name. She wrote Doris Plumber and passed the chart to the person seated behind her. Jules nodded, said: "Well, Doris, welcome to the search for a theme. What do you believe one of our themes should be?"

Doris looked embarrassed at having been called on so soon. She wished she had selected a seat farther down the row. "I think how women have fought for equality is an important theme."

"And right you are," Jules replied. "Suffrage was granted to women by the 17th Amendment in 1919-20, but it had already been implemented in many states before that date. Who were some of the noted leaders of the movement, past and present? For example, who was Emma Willard, and what were her accomplishments? She would make a good topic for a term paper."

The seating chart returned to the front of the third row. A male African-American student was seated in the front desk. Jules pointed to the square where he wished for him to sign. The student signed his name, Malcolm Kenyatta. "Malcolm," Jules said, "let me guess. Do you wish to look at the theme of racism in American society?"

Malcolm gave Jules a skeptical look. "Would you have asked me that question if my skin were white?"

Oh, holy shit! Jules knew he had blown it. How to backtrack his mistaken statement? "Sorry, your right, I shouldn't have asked that question—not in that way. Sometimes, even when we have the best of intentions, we screw up. Because we look like we belong to a particular group of people, others assume certain stereotypical things about us. I'm Jewish. People assume all Jewish men wear a skullcap, Kippah, and have a prayer shawl, Tallit. And of course all Jews attend a synagogue. I don't do any of those things. Stereotypes are part of racist thinking. Again, I'm sorry for having misspoken."

Malcolm looked Jules in the eye and replied: "Accepted."

The seating chart arrived at the top of the fourth row. The seat was taken by a young man who looked like he had just come off the football field, Duke Blue Devils jersey and all. Jules said to himself—let's see if I can avoid screwing this one up too. The student wrote his name in the square, Mike McDonald. Jules looked down at the bulky figure filling the chair in front of him and said: "Glad to see you mike. What did you do on your summer vacation?"

Mike stretched out as if he was preparing to give a lengthy answer to Jules's question. "Well, I'll tell you, Mr. Stein. My older brother bought a new Jeep. He wanted to test it out on some rough roads. So we took a trip to Alaska. Talk about rough roads. We really experienced them. Mile after mile of nothing but gravel. When we got to Anchorage, we went to visit some glaciers. I am glad we did. They are all melting. The park rangers told us that the temperature in Alaska is rising far faster than it is in North Carolina. In a few years there won't be any glaciers left. I believe one of the themes we should look at is global warming. What can we do to save the planet?"

"That certainly is worth looking at," Jules replied. "How did we get ourselves into such a sorry state of affairs? It can all be traced back to the industrial revolution and the burning of fossil fuels. What will be our source of energy in the future?"

The seating chart had now arrived at the top of the final row. A girl with a studious look about her—hair, eyes, dress—was perched lightly on the front seat. Jules pointed to the appropriate square for her to sign. She wrote Beverly Eagleton. Jules was about to ask her for a theme when she looked up and spoke to him directly, saying: "Mr. Stein, you have been asking us all of the questions. I think it is about time you answered a few of our questions. Here you are—a doctoral student at Duke University. Which historical themes do you personally favor? What is the theoretical perspective through which you view the world?"

Jules was taken back. He wasn't prepared for a scholarly question coming from an undergraduate student. How to reply? "That is a very perceptive question. You must come from an academic family."

"Yes," Beverly replied, "my father is a professor of philosophy at Chapel Hill."

"Good, let me see if I can give you a short answer to a long question. I think the study of history is part of our quest for meaning. We look at the past in order to reconstruct a sequence of events aimed at helping us to better understand the present. Further, I believe one of the perennial themes running through human history is the belief in superstitions. What is a superstition? It is nothing more than a false idea that is dreamed up in order to explain what otherwise seems unexplainable. What makes the world go around? One of these root explanations is what we can call the puppet and puppeteer metaphor. People are mere puppets and someone or some force is the puppeteer. Who is pulling your strings? The Puritan who settled in colonial New England believed in an all-knowing, all-powerful God. All the events in the world were predestined to occur in exactly the way they unfolded. Freedom of will

124

was an illusion. Only the God-fearing Puritans would be saved." Jules smiled, adding, "Let me tell you a little ditty. It runs something like this: We are the sweet and selected few; let all the rest be damned. There is room enough in hell for them; we don't want heaven crammed." Some of the students laughed. "The story of the puppeteer does not end with the Puritans. Marx believed history followed laws. Central to his philosophy of dialectical materialism was the concept of economic modes of production. Everything in society, the whole of its social superstructure, was determined by its economic substructure. We are all puppets controlled by the economic forces around us. The puppeteer, if we read Freud, is lurking in the depths of our own minds. The unconscious mind is pulling the strings-- determining why we make the choices we make. The story does not end there. Look at behaviorism. Skinner believes the secret to constructing a human being lies in operant conditioning. Puppet and puppeteer." Jules paused to look around the room. What confronted him was row after row of empty faces. Clearly he had missed the mark—told his students more than they were ready to learn. He felt just like a puppeteer who had lost his puppets.

....

Jules poured himself a cup of coffee and followed Professor Peterson across the cafeteria. They stopped at a table next to a window, where an elderly man was seated all by himself. He was reading an article in the *Scientific American.*

"Mind if we join you?" Professor Peterson asked, setting his cup of coffee on the table.

A pair of thick rimmed glasses looked up from the journal. "No, not at all, please join me."

"I don't believe you have met Mr. Stein," Professor Peterson offered. "He's one of our doctoral students, and he's teaching a class for us this fall. Jules, this is Professor Yoshioka. He's in theoretical physics."

A small hand with delicate fingers was extended toward Jules.

"I understand you have been nominated for a Nobel Prize," Professor Peterson said, seating himself at the table and gesturing for Jules to do the same.

Yoshioka smiled, nodded. "A twenty-year project."

Jules glanced at the title of the article Professor Yoshioka had been reading: Is the Universe Finite or Infinite? "Which is it?" he asked.

Professor Yoshioka smiled. "Take your choice. Given the theory of the Big Bang, it is definitely finite, but it is expanding into infinity."

Professor Peterson laughed, saying: "We always used to look at physics as the model of a hard science. Reality is reality; truth is truth. Whatever happened?"

Yoshioka leaned back in his chair—running his slender fingers over the balding spot on top of his head. "Physics is not the discipline it was fifty years ago. Our whole conception of the nature of the universe has changed. The hard and fast laws of Newton have given way to Heisenberg and the capricious theories of quantum mechanics."

"What is quantum mechanics anyway?" Jules asked.

Professor Yoshioka flashed a smile at Professor Peterson, replied: "You need to enroll in one of my classes."

The two professors laughed.

"I read where Einstein claimed his Theory of Relativity first came to him as an intuition. Do you think that was the case?'

Professor Yoshioka raised his hands as if to surrender, replied: "Who am I to question Einstein? If he said it was an intuition, then that is what it was. The man was a genius. He gave us a new way of looking at the universe that no one had dreamed was possible." Professor Yoshioka removed his thick glasses and rubbed the bridge of his nose. "I wish he were around today. We could certainly use his insight into dark matter and dark energy." He laughed more to himself than with the other two men seated at the table. "If, when I was a doctoral student, I had told my professors that most of the universe was missing, they would have laughed me out of the program. Yet here we are—trying to find evidence of dark matter and dark energy so we can try to determine if they are responsible for why the universe is expanding faster than the speed of light."

"I didn't think anything could travel faster than the speed of light," Jules offered, a note of puzzlement in his voice.

"That is correct within the universe itself, but on its outer edges it is expanding faster than the speed of light." Yoshioka laughed, added: "The universe is a place filled with strange paradoxes, and it gets stranger every day. Subatomic particle can only be said to exist when we are there looking for them."

"I've been reading Hawking's *A Brief History of Time*," Jules asserted. "Do you believe there is probably a black hole at the center of every galaxy?"

"The evidence seems to support that idea," Professor Yoshioka noted.

"Jules is dealing with a black hole problem of his own. He wants to write his dissertation on superstition, specifically a place in the woods not far from here known as the Devil's Tramping Ground." Professor Peterson asked: "Have you ever heard of the place?"

"The Devil's Tramping Ground, no," Professor Yoshioka replied, shaking his head. "But superstitions, yes, we have had plenty of them in the history of science. Aristotle left us with the belief that our neighboring planets were gods and therefore had to move in perfect circles—a belief that lasted until Kepler came along and showed us evidence that planets move in ellipses. We can also look at the recent fad surrounding string theory, which now appears to be dead because of a lack of empirical evidence. Superstitions are merely popular beliefs accepted at face value without any supporting evidence. They are the black holes of the mind. Superstition is like believing Donald Trump won the 2020 election."

The three men around the table all laughed openly.

. . . .

"Jules," Professor Peterson said, stepping outside his office, "can I see you for a minute?"

"I was just on my way to class."

Professor Peterson gave Jules an earnest look, said: "That's what I wanted to talk with you about."

Jules seated himself across the desk from his major professor. There was a sense of formality in the air. Jules knew something was sorely wrong. He had been around universities long enough to detect that feeling—a feeling of a personal chill—a feeling of when one man pulls superior rank on another man. Jules prepared himself for the worst.

Professor Peterson began. "Jules, I think I should let you know I received a complaint from one of your students."

Jules' heart sank.

"The young woman stopped by my office earlier today to let me know she was dropping your class."

Jules pressed his moist palms tightly against the legs of his trousers.

"She told me she was dropping your class because she didn't think she was getting out of the class what it was intended to offer."

"I see," Jules said, his words were flat and lifeless.

"Her main complaint, however, was ledged against your teaching style. She said you were abrasive and sarcastic with your students."

The blood drained from Jules' face.

"I asked her if she could give me a specific example of when you had been insulting. She said she couldn't recall any single case, but it was more a matter of your whole general attitude."

Jules shook his head, replied: "I guess I may have leaned on them a little too hard, but I was merely trying to get them to think about the meaning of historical events."

Professor Peterson leaned back in his swivel chair. His mood suddenly softened. "Don't take it too hard. It's not a federal case. We get complaints all the time. I called

you in because I thought you needed to know."

Jules tried to smile, offered apologetically: "Maybe

I came on too strong. I guess I could back off a little. I was

just trying to keep them awake and thinking."

Professor Peterson smiled, said lightly: "Before she

left she told me she was a member of the Church of Christ.

She said she had never met anyone before who was so

down on religion. She said she thought you were the Anti-

Christ."

Both men laughed.

"Oh, Jules, there is one more thing. Professor

Yoshioka sent me a note to deliver to you." Professor

Peterson handed Jules an envelope containing a single sheet

of paper. "He said he thought you might want to check out

these three men. You might find them helpful in writing

your dissertation on the Devil's Tramping Ground."

Jules opened the envelope and looked at the three names scribbled on the sheet of paper. They were: Dr. Clark, Soil Chemical Analysis at N. C. State; Dr. Oliver, Neutron Laboratory, N. C. State; and Dr. Davidson, Gravity Measurement Laboratory, Chapel Hill. Jules had never heard of any of them, but he knew he needed to contact all three.

....

Jules pulled his Volkswagen off the highway and onto a drive leading to a single story brick building. There was a sign out front reading: North Carolina Department of Agriculture, Soil Testing Division. Jules left his car and walked to the entrance of the building, taking with him the two paper bags of dirt from the Devil's Tramping Ground.

Entering the building, Jules confronted a secretary seated behind a large oak desk. "Can I help you?" she asked.

"Yes, I'm Mr. Stein. I called the other day—asked about having some soil tested."

"Have you filled out one of our green forms?"

"No."

"We'll have to have a green form before we can process your samples."

Jules took the green form and seated himself on a couch that was located next to the secretary's desk. He hated forms—hated them with a passion. They represented the bureaucratic mentality of modern society, more needless questions. "Excuse me," Jules said, addressing himself to the secretary. "Do I need to answer all of these questions? I mean, when it asks me what I plan to plant next season. Well, you see, I don't plan on planting anything. I just want to have the soil analyzed."

The secretary gave Jules a hard, questioning look. "Oh, you have a special problem. All special problems are required to fill out our yellow form." She handed Jules a bright yellow form.

Jules looked at the questions. They were as irrelevant as those on the green form. What to do? Finally, he asked: "Would it be possible for me to speak with the agronomist?"

The secretary flashed Jules an indignant look as if to say: Who do you think you are? She picked up the phone—pressed some buttons—talked softly—returned the phone to its place on the desk. "Dr. Clark says he will see you." Pointing down the hall, she added: "Third door on the right."

Dr. Clark was a tall, slender man with a gray mustache. His office smelled of aromatic pipe tobacco. A well-burned meerschaum pipe lay on the desk.

"I'm Mr. Stein," Jules said, extending his hand across the desk.

"P. Clark," the agronomist replied, meeting Jules' hand over the middle of the desk.

"I have a special problem." Jules began.

"That's what I understand."

"Neither of your forms fit my particular situation. I'm working on my dissertation at Duke. I'm writing it on A History of Superstitions Surrounding the Devil's Tramping Ground. Have you heard of the place?"

"Yes," Dr. Clark smiled, nodded. "That certainly sounds like a dissertation title."

"Anyway, I'd like to have a test run on the soil inside the circle—find out why nothing grows there. I have some soil samples I have brought with me—both inside and outside the circle."

Dr. Clark reached for his pipe. "You would like to know what the chemical composition of the soil is, but you are not interested in knowing what you would have to add in order to make something grow."

"That's right."

Dr. Clark struck a match, touching it to the bowl of his pipe. Glancing at the paper bags Jules had brought with him, he asked: "Are those your samples?"

Jules placed the bags on the desk. "Yes, I have them marked, inside and outside."

"How many cores did you take for each sample?"

"Cores?"

"Yes, we usually recommend fifteen."

"I selected soil from a number of different places both inside and outside the circle."

Dr. Clark smiled, striking another match. "We probably have enough for a reliable test—given the purposes you have in mind."

"That would be great."

Dr. Clark puffed slowly on his pipe as if deep in thought. Finally he asked: "Would you like to take a look at our lab?"

Jules nodded. "Yes, very much."

The two men walked down a long hall and through a door marked RECEIVING.

"This is where all the samples come," Dr. Clark explained. "We begin by assigning each one a permanent identification number. Then the samples are dried in a warm air drier, crushed and sieved." He opened the door to a closet lined with rows of little brown boxes. "From here the sample goes to our lab." The two men passed through a pair of heavy swinging doors and into a large room filled with test tubes, beakers, hoses, and the pungent smell of acid. "We make seven basic tests on every sample. The pH test for acidity or alkalinity probably tells us more about the fertility of a soil than any other single test."

"I guess the problem in North Carolina is too much acid in the soils," Jules said, trying to appear somewhat informed about the topic.

That's right. We have to add lime in order to get things to grow. In the western United States they face exactly the opposite problem, too much alkali." Dr. Clark stopped in front of a large piece of electronic equipment. "Here is where we test for organic matter. This test is performed by chemically burning a measure of the soil with acid. The burned organic matter within the soil turns green. We use this colorimeter to give us a reading on the amount of organic matter present."

"I'll bet you don't find very much matter in my sample," Jules said in a joking manner.

"There is always some organic matter present. It doesn't matter how barren your soil is. You can't defeat mother nature."

The two men walked to the other side of the lab. "Here is where we test for the five different nutrient elements—calcium, phosphorus, potassium, magnesium, and manganese. We prepare an extract by adding a diluted solution of hydrochloric and sulfuric acid to a measure of soil. Then we place the mixture on our shaker for exactly five minutes. The potassium content is read on a flame photometer. The calcium, magnesium, and manganese contents are each read by an atomic adsorption spectrophotometer." Dr. Clark walked to a shinny piece of equipment. "This is our new spectrophotometer. We had to shell out eighty thousand dollars for it. The machine works on the principle of when an element is burned in a standard gas flame it gives off a particular wave length of light. The spectrophotometer measures that light."

Jules shook his head, asked: "Who thinks up all of this stuff?"

Dr. Clark laughed, replied: "We've been working on the process of a good many years. We've pretty well gotten soil analysis down to a science."

"What if one of your tests doesn't turn out right— gives you a faulty reading?"

Dr. Clark smiled, shook his head. "That rarely happens. And even when it does we have a way of catching it. One out of every thirty-six samples in line is a check sample with a known reading. If the analysis on that sample does not agree with the known value, then we run the whole batch back through the process again." He fished in his pocket and came up with another match, striking it and lighting his pipe, he added: "Don't worry, Mr. Stein, when we're finished with your samples, we will have found your devil for you."

....

It was a bright, sunny fall day. Just the kind of day when it is good to be alive. That morning Jules had gotten in his car and driven the twenty miles from Durham to Raleigh. He had turned off of the beltline running around the city and followed the signs leading to North Carolina State University. At the entrance he had picked up a visitor's parking sticker and inquired about the location of the Nuclear Energy Services. The dark-eyed girl in the information booth had shown him the location on the university map. It was a low-lying, red brick building in the middle of the campus. Jules had parked his car and walked to the appointed building. At just that moment he was standing in a small office filling out a card for a radiation badge.

"Where should I pin this?" Jules asked the secretary.

"Why don't you pin it to your shirt pocket," the secretary suggested. "I'll call Dr. Oliver and let him know you've arrived."

Jules stood, waited, looked around the room, studied the way the secretary filled out her light blue sweater.

"Hope we haven't kept you waiting too long." The words came from a short, balding man dressed in a white smock.

"No, I just arrived."

"From our conversation on the phone, I wasn't quite sure what you were interested in seeing."

Jules fidgeted uneasily. He wasn't quite sure either. "I understand you are able to analyze the atomic structure of things. I'd like to know a little more about how your process works."

"Well, if that's the case, why don't I give you a general tour of our lab."

The two men walked down a winding hall until they came to a tiled room with a large piece of plate glass built into one wall. There, through the plate glass, located a floor below them, was a nuclear reactor.

"This is our Pulstar Reactor," Dr. Oliver explained. "It's one of the swimming pool variety. The nuclear fuel is built into metal rods which are held in a framework at the bottom of the pool. The water serves as a shield to protect us from radiation as well as to slow down the neutrons that we use to bombard our target atoms."

"Is it turned on right now?" Jules asked, glancing nervously at the SCRAM procedures posted on the wall.

"No, we only run it for short intervals."

Jules peered down into the pool of water, asked: "How long have you had the reactor?"

"The program began some fifty years ago. Our services are very specialized. There are only two other labs that offer services similar to ours. We are the only university in the country to offer services to both government and industry on a full-time basis. We now analyze between a hundred and a hundred and fifty samples a week."

"Can you analyze the atomic structure of anything?"

"Yes, virtually anything you would care to give us. Neutron Activation Analysis can tell us what the precise elements are in a given sample. Perhaps you remember from your chemistry class that the nuclei of atoms are stable only when they contain a certain number of neutrons and protons. The number of protons in an atom's nucleus determines its identity. The number of neutrons usually tells us whether or not the atom is radioactive. The fact that nuclei can absorb additional neutrons—converting a stable element into a radioactive one—makes Neutron Activation Analysis possible."

"Does your reactor add neutrons to the nuclei of the atoms?" Jules was trying hard to recall the little he had once memorized about chemistry.

"That's right. We bombard an atom with neutrons, altering its atomic weight and causing it to emit gamma rays."

"How do you detect the gamma rays?"

"That's the second step in our operation. Follow me downstairs and I'll show you."

The two men left the reactor—passing through a set of heavy wooden doors and down a long flight of stairs leading to a small room filled with electronic equipment.

"This is a gamma-ray spectrometer," Dr. Oliver explained, walking over to a steel box. "It incorporates a lithium-drifted germanium crystal as a detector. The data we gather here is fed into our pulse-height analyzer."

Jules nodded as if he understood all Dr. Oliver was telling him.

"Because radioactive nuclei decay at different rates," Dr. Oliver continued, "each yields a distinct pattern of radiation. Measurement of these radiations can determine the kind and number of radioactive atoms that are present. The lead shield you see here helps to screen out most of the gamma rays that come from the naturally radioactive materials in this room. The large container here at the bottom is a reservoir of liquid nitrogen. It keeps the detector cooled to a temperature of -196 degrees centigrade."

"I'm afraid you've gone way beyond my basic chemistry class," Jules admitted reluctantly.

Dr. Oliver smiled, adding: "Stick with me a minute more. We not only do basic research, but we work on some very practical problems as well. The other day the local sheriff's office brought us a sample of marijuana. He wanted to know whether it was locally grown or an imported product. We ran it through our process and were able to tell him from the traces of soil that were attached to the plant that it was a home-grown sample. Last year we had a case brought to us by the telephone company. Thieves had been shooting down the copper wire and selling it for scrap. The company thought they knew who was stealing the wire, but they didn't have enough proof to make a case stick in court. We were able to take samples from the salvage yard wire and match it with the wire from the phone company. The uses for Neutron Activation Analysis are virtually limitless."

"Could you make an analysis of the elements present in a sample of soil?"

"Sure, we do that all the time."

Jules paused, pondering his next question. Did he have the moxie to ask Dr. Oliver to analyze the samples of soil from the Devil's Tramping Ground he had left in the car?

....

"You must be Mr. Stein."

"That's right," Jules replied, extending his hand in greeting.

Jules' hand was grasped by Stewart Davidson, who was Professor of Geophysics at the University of North Carolina in Chapel Hill. Davidson was one of the counties foremost authorities on earthquakes. He had been instrumental in getting the university to install one of the most sophisticated seismographs in the eastern United States.

"Hope we haven't kept you waiting long."

"Not at all," Jules replied. "I just got here a few minutes ago." Jules pointed to a poster on the wall in Davidson's office. "Are those the Alps?"

151

"Yes, lovely valley isn't it. I visited there a few years ago. Fell in love with the place. Too bad they don't build universities in places like that."

"The mountains look like they rise straight up from the valley. It must have taken some powerful geological forces to shape the valley."

"It is all a matter of plate tectonics," Professor Davidson replied.

"I hope to visit Switzerland sometime."

"Well, Mr. Stein, what is it that we can do for you?"

"I'm working on a doctorate at Duke. I want to write my dissertation on the superstitions surrounding the Devil's Tramping Ground. Have you heard of the place?"

"Isn't that where the football team takes their dates in order scare the pants off of them? I understand there have been a number of reported rapes out there as well." Professor Davidson said lightly.

"I wouldn't know about that," Jules replied, smiling.

"You are doing research on the Devil's Tramping Ground. How can we be of service to you?"

"Over the years there have been a lot of stories told about the place. I am interested in showing that the stories are all baseless superstitions. So much of what the popular mind believes to be true is merely superstition. For example, all the stuff you see on TV about ancient aliens."

Professor Davidson laughed. "So you want to take on all the myth makers. What you need are a few scientific tools if you hope to put a dint in ignorance. Let me show you a few we have accumulated here at the university."

"That would be great."

"Have you seen our seismograph?'

"Was it the drum in the glass case when I come in the front door?"

153

"That's half of it. The other half—the rods—are buried outside of town. They are so sensitive that if we had them at the university all we would record would be traffic vibrations." Professor Davidson stood and walked to an adjacent door. "If you'd like to come into the lab, I'll show you some of our new equipment."

Jules followed the geophysicist across the hall and into a large room. It was stacked high with a wide assortment of maps, graphs, charts, and electronic equipment. Professor Davidson picked up a long roll of paper covered with scratchy lines. "This is from our seismograph upstairs. It recorded the day the earthquake hit Alaska." Pointing to a series of oscillating lines, he added: "Here is where we picked up the P-wave. There is where we began to get the S-wave. Later the PP-wave and the SS-wave are both arriving. It was a fairly deep quake. Ninety percent of all earthquakes have their hypocenters forty-five to fifty miles below the earth's crust."

154

Jules looked at the mass of squiggly lines. He didn't know the difference between a P-wave and an S-wave, but it was clear something big was happening. "How strong was the quake?"

"It was a beauty—6.2 on the Richter scale." Professor Davidson added with a smile. "About the size of quake I am predicting for Willington."

"I see in the newspaper where you've told Carolina Power they shouldn't build a nuclear plan down there on the coast. The area is located on a fault."

"Yes, but they're hell-bent on doing it anyway. Wilmington is one of the most geologically active areas on the east coast. If you were to ask a panel of geologists to pick the worst spot to locate a nuclear plant, the unqualified first choice would be Wilmington."

"I thought North Carolina was supposed to be a relatively stable zone."

"Stable!" Professor Davidson's voice rose in pitch. "It's anything but stable. It is a virtual honeycomb of fault lines. We're in for a major quake—mark my words—and no one wants to listen. All Carolina Power can think about is how to turn on another kilowatt. Well, let them build their nuclear plant—let them place it right on top of a fault line—then there'll be hell to pay."

"Can't anything be done to stop them?"

"Not really. It's all politics and money."

Jules shook his head. "That's a shame."

Davidson extracted another sheet of graph paper from the pile. "This reading is from yesterday. We have the drum set on a twenty-four hour cycle." He pointed to a series of small fluctuating lines. "This is from about twelve o'clock last night. These vibrations show someone drove out to the enclosure and stopped his car. Here is where he got out and walked over to the fence, stood for a minute and looked at it, returned to the car and slammed the door, stared the engine, and drove away."

Jules laughed. "You can tell all that."

"The police are supposed to stop and check on the fence every night. If they miss a night, we can catch them on the graph the next day. They don't like it much—our keeping tabs on them."

"Do you have a smaller seismograph—something that can be used in the field?"

Professor Davidson nodded. "We have a number of different devices." He walked to a closet and returned with a hand meter and a sledge hammer. "This is the simplest kind of seismograph. The sledge hammer has some wires attached here at the end. What you do is carry the meter down field, say a hundred yards, then you have someone slam the sledge down on a piece of steel plate. The meter measures the length of time it takes the shock wave to arrive."

"What can that tell you?"

"What we are looking for is an anomaly—a shift from a regular reading. Shockwaves travel faster through dense material such as rock."

Jules studied the seismograph. This, he thought to himself, I understand.

Professor Davidson returned to his closet and came back with an electric box and a long coil of wire. "Here is a slightly more sophisticated example of the same thing. We call it the dynamite seismograph. You spread out the wires and then set off your charge. It can give a much clearer picture of what you happen to be standing on."

"Let me ask you something," Jules said. "The last time I was at the Smithsonian Institution in Washington I found out that the earth's gravity is not uniform. Some places have stronger gravity than others. Do you have something for measuring gravity?"

Professor Davidson nodded and opened a padded box, removing a metal cylinder. He placed it gently on the table. "We have to be very careful with this instrument. It's delicately balanced. This particular gravimeter is new—cost a hundred thousand dollars."

"That much!" Jules looked surprised.

"Yes, and believe it or not, the expense is all in one little spring, which has to be made by hand. There's no way to mass produce them. They may have to make as many as a thousand springs before they get one that is just right." Professor Davidson peered into a small peek hole at the top of the cylinder.

"What kind of gravity reading do you get in Chapel Hill?"

"Gravity is read in gals and milligals. Everything in North Carolina falls within the range of 979.000 to 980.000 gals."

"What are the highest and lowest readings on earth?"

Professor Davidson continued peering into the holes and to adjusting two silver knobs. "The poles have the highest readings, the equator has the lowest."

"Why is that?"

"The earth is not a perfect sphere. It bulges in the middle and flattens out at the poles—the effects of centrifugal force. Consequently, the poles are closer to the center of the earth."

"What kind of reading would you get at the equator?"

Professor Davidson looked up from the instrument. "The equator is 978 gals, the poles are 983. We could use this particular instrument at the equator but not at the poles. Its calibration does not go beyond 982 gals. If you would like to look into the peep holes, you can see where the beam of light intersects with the crosshairs."

Jules placed his eye on the instrument. He saw the light and the crosshairs and where the two came together, but he still did not know what he was looking at.

"We are standing at 979 gals right now. If we were to move up one floor, the instrument would be able to measure the difference—one tenth of a milligal per foot. That's how sensitive it is."

Jules looked around the room at all of the scientific devices. He had seen all he was interested in. A hollow pit formed in his stomach. It was now or never for him to pop the question—the real reason it had come to Chapel Hill. "I wonder," Jules began hesitantly. "if you ever lend out any of your equipment to graduate students. I could make good use of some of your instruments."

Professor Davidson gave Jules a skeptical look, like you must be kidding. "No, that never happens. It's all too expensive and too hard to replace." Then sensing Jules' disappointment, he added: "Though I might meet you at your Devil's Tramping Ground some Saturday, and we could measure what the dynamite seismograph tells us about the place."

....

Jules spread the daily mail out on the kitchen table. There was the usual assortment of bills, advertisements, and magazines. Two envelopes caught his eye. Both came from North Carolina State University, one from the Department of Agriculture and the other from the Nuclear Energy Services. Excitedly, Jules opened the letter from the Department of Agriculture first.

North Carolina Department of Agriculture

Soil Testing Division

Dear Mr. Stein:

We were pleased to test the soil samples you

left with us. We are always glad to lend our assistance to an interested researcher. Below you will find a breakdown of the chemical composition we found in your samples.

	Inside Circle	Outside Circle
Acidity	5.8	4.4
Organic Matter	.2	3.5
Pounds Per Acre		
Calcium	1100	200
Magnesium	1000	330
Phosphors	75	2.5
Potassium	160	35
Manganese	17	3
Nitrate nitrogen ppm	1	1
Soluble Salts index	4	0

Looking at the chemical breakdown of your samples, any soil scientist would have to agree that the soil within the circle certainly ought to support many different forms of plant life.

Indeed, the soil within the circle is really much

better suited for plant growth than the soil

outside the circle. As you will note, we found

very little organic matter to be present in the

sample that came from inside the circle. Such

a low reading is highly unusual. One would

almost think that the soil had been chemically

sterilized, except we found no traces of any

chemicals. Why doesn't plant life flourish

inside the circle? Who the Devil knows!

Sincerely yours,

Rogers P. Clark

Agronomist

....

The second envelope was opened as quickly as the

first. Jules was eager to see what the Nuclear Laboratory

would say about his soil samples. Would there be any new truth about the Devil's Tramping Ground?

Nuclear Energy Services

Dear Mr. Stein:

Below you will find the results of our analysis of the soil samples you left with us. We hope you will find them useful in your research. Kindly let us know if we can be of further service.

Elements	Inside Circle	Outside Circle
Sb	0.32	0.59
As	4.1	2.3
Br	7.1	6.2
Cr	76.3	31.4
Co	17.2	9.6
Eu	3.1	6.2
Fe	61,200	36,500
La	36.9	42.3

Mn	2100	1716
Hg	.10	.11
Sm	22.2	19.7
Sc	14.2	9.7
Na	11,100	10,900
Zn	110	114
U	4.2	2.9
Alpha Active	18.8	11.5
Beta Active	385	226

Summary. The samples you furnished us from inside the circle show some very remarkable properties. The Alpha and Beta readings are unusually high. There is nothing, however, that tells us why no vegetation grows in the circle.

Sincerely yours,

Bill Oliver

Head, Nuclear Services Laboratory

....

Jules had arrived early. He had parked his Volkswagen just off the highway—adjacent to the trail leading to the Devil's Tramping Ground. Professor Davidson had called the day before—said he would meet him there at 10:30 AM. It might be a good idea if Jules brought along a shovel. You never know when you may have to do a little digging. Jules looked into his rearview mirror—checked his watch—wished he had brought along a book to read. What is it they say about time when you are waiting for something to happen? The watched pot never boils.

A car suddenly moved in behind Jules. Turning in his seat, Jules could see it was Professor Davidson. Glancing at his watch, he noted that it was exactly 10:30. Jules left his car and walked back to greet Professor Davidson.

"Have you been waiting long?" Professor Davidson asked.

"Not long," Jules replied.

"Help me get some equipment we will be using out of the trunk."

When the trunk was opened there was the dynamite seismograph, several carefully wrapped sticks of dynamite, and an auger for digging nice neat little holes in the ground. "I'll take the seismography and the dynamite," Professor Davidson explained. "You bring the auger and your shovel. I hope you brought your shovel."

"Yes, I have it in my car."

"Great, well, show me where we go. I can't wait to see this Devil's Tramping Ground."

Jules picked up the auger and his shovel and started up the trail through the woods. He was followed closely by Professor Davidson. The sun shown down through the pines—creating contorted shadows on the ground. Jules

168

wished he had brought a camera. The shadows, he thought, would make an interesting Rorschach Test. Jules smiled to himself—remembering an old story about the ink blots. A man went to take the Rorschach Ink Blot Test. The psychologist showed him the first picture and asked the man what he saw. The man replied: I see a man trying to make it on his own. The psychologist showed the man the second picture. The man replied: I see a man and woman making it together. The third ink blot was shown to the man. This time he exclaimed: Lord, they are all having an orgy! With that the psychologist turned to the man and asked: Is sex all you have on your mind? To which the man replied: Well, Doc, you're the one who keeps showing me all the dirty pictures.

Shortly, Jules and Professor Davidson came to the swampy place on the trail. They made their way across by carefully stepping on a couple of fallen logs. Having gotten across the swamp, they came in view of the circle with its distorted trees.

"So this is the famous Devil's Tramping Ground," Professor Donaldson mused.

"This is it. Not a very impressive sight. Looks like some group had a beer party out here. They threw their beer cans all around." Jules kicked a couple of cans off of the circle.

"Well, let's see if we can unlock some of its secrets."

"I hope to show that there are scientific and historical reasons for why people selected this spot to serve as a center for their superstitions. I hope to weave science and history into a theoretical matrix for unlocking superstitions."

"Wow! Is that all? Be sure and send me a copy of your dissertation when you've finished it."

The two men laughed.

Professor Davidson made a visual survey of the surrounding forest. "The trees and undergrowth are pretty compact around the circle. It won't be easy to get a good measurement form our seismograph, but we will give it a shot." Looking at Jules, he instructed, "See if you can dig me two holes using the auger. One about 20 paces south of the circle and the other 20 paces west. Dig them nice and deep so the dynamite can be covered with dirt. I'll lay out the lines from the holes to the seismograph over here."

With that the two men got to work—each to his appointed task. Shortly the holes were dug and dynamite was place in the south hole. "Are you ready?" Professor Davidson asked. "It is easier to set off a charge electronically today than it was back in the good old days when you had to light a fuse and run." With that there was a loud bang and a cloud of dirt was blown into the air. "That was a nice wave," Professor Davidson exclaimed.

"I would say, just off hand, that there is some kind of anomaly running through your circle. We can tell a bit more about it when we set off the other charge."

Jules watched as Professor Davidson placed the stick of dynamite in the second hole. "Now use your shovel to cover it up. Then stand back and we'll call fire in the hole."

Both men laughed at the last line.

The dynamite charge was ignited. Again there was a roar and dirt few in the air. "Excellent," Professor Davidson exclaimed. "that was a good clear wave. Just as I thought, there is some typed of anomaly running through the circle. I can't tell you how deep or exactly what it is, but something is clearly there. Jules, if you have the time you might dig a few test holes around in the circle. I have a feeling whatever it is isn't buried deeply. And, oh yes, when I get back into the office, I'll write up a report of what we've found. You may wish to stick it in the appendix to your dissertation. Doctoral committees love to see some

empirical data."

Chapter 4

The Maelstrom

It was a grand day for a birthday party. Chucky Stein was two-years-old. All the members of his family— mother, father, grandmother, and grandfather were gathered around the kitchen table. Everyone had brought Chucky a brightly wrapped gift. The family was presently engaged in unwrapping what Chucky had received.

"Oh, look, Chucky," Jennifer said, addressing herself to her son who was seated in his highchair. "See what your grandfather bought for your birthday." She handed a bright red popgun to Chucky, who took it in one hand and struck it down hard on his eating try causing the gun to drop to the floor. Chucky looked down as if being surprised and disappointed.

"I've got it," Jules said, reaching down and retrieving the popgun and placing it on the table. "I had one very much like it when I was a little kid. I don't remember who bought it for me." Looking at Chucky, he added, "You are not quite ready to go hunting yet."

"Ok, Chucky, let's unwrap this one," Jennifer said, picking up a bright orange package with a large brown bow. "And who is it from? You guessed it; it is from your mother." Jennifer carefully removed the wrapping paper from the package—paying particular attention to saving its bow. "What do we have inside? Why there is a collection of storybooks. See here is one about *Little Red Riding Hood*, and another about *Jack and the Beanstalk,* and this one was my favorite when I was a little girl, *Snow White and the Seven Dwarves*. Won't we have fun reading these along with the other fairy-tales?"

Chucky smiled, made little sounds of pleasure, and reached out for the bright pictures on the books. Jennifer held them up for Chucky to see, but she held them back from his outstretched hands. "We need to keep them clean for now," she said.

Jules had already started unwrapping the present he had given Chucky. Everyone strained to see what he had bought. When all the paper had been removed, Jules set a dark green box on the table.

What's in the box?" Grace asked.

"It's a collection of Montessori instructional activities for young children," Jules replied.

"Who was Montessori?" Charles asked.

"She was an Italian physician and educator who developed a method of instruction that allowed children not only to develop tactual skills but intellectual process as well. It is never too soon to start focusing on a child's cognitive abilities."

"Oh, Jules," Jennifer remarked, "he is just a baby. Can't his brain wait until he goes to Kindergarten? Childhood is a time for having fun."

"Let's unwrap what I bought for Chucky," Grace insisted. "I think he is going to like it. We purchased one for Jennifer when she was two. She pulled it after her everywhere she went."

"Oh, no," Jennifer said laughing. "You didn't buy him a Quaky-Duck."

Jules took hold of the duck and pushed it across the table to Chucky, whose face lit up with surprise and interest. The quack, quack of the duck particularly caught his attention. Chucky squirmed in his highchair and reached out for the Duck.

"See," Grace replied, a note of self-satisfaction in her voice, "he really likes what I gave him."

Chucky pulled the duck onto his feeding tray and began to push it back and forth.

Jennifer smiled. "Clearly the duck is his favorite toy."

"Isn't it time we lit the candles on the cake?" Charles asked, having spied the cake the moment he set foot in the apartment.

"Oh, Dad," Jennifer said, "you are such a big kid."

"Well, your father has always loved your cakes. And chocolate is his favorite." Looking at Jules as if to explain what she was about to say, Grace added: "Jennifer was born knowing how to bake cakes. When she was a little girl we bought her an Easy Bake Ovens with a light bulb inside. She was always baking up something. Isn't that right, Charles?"

"Oh, mother, you don't have to tell everyone all of those old stories," Jennifer protested.

"Let's get this whole show on the road," Jules interjected, placing two large candles in the top of the cake and lighting them with his cigar lighter.

"Shouldn't we all sing happy birthday before cutting the cake?" Grace asked.

"You're absolutely right mother. Let's all sing happy birthday to Chucky."

While the candles burned on top of the cake, the adults around the table and began singing: "Happy birthday to you; happy birthday to you; happy birthday dear Chucky; happy birthday to you. And many more!"

Chucky laughed, slapping his hands down on his eating tray. His childish noises indicated his pleasure with what was taking place around the table. And who wouldn't be pleased—being the center of attention.

"Ok," Jennifer said, "everyone make a wish for Chucky." There was a moment of silence. Then she added:

"On the count of three, everyone help blow out the candles. Ready—Set—one, two, three, blow." Everyone blew in the direction of the cake. One candle refused to go out!

....

The iPhone was playing its catchy little tune for the third time. Someone clearly wanted to speak with Jennifer Stein. Half-way through the tune, Jennifer picked up her phone and said, "Hello."

"Oh, Jennifer, I hoped I would catch you. I have been meaning to call you like forever—hoping we could get caught up on things. I hope you're not too busy to talk."

"No, Chucky is taking his nap, and I was just sitting here at my dressing table putting on some Bobbie Brown makeup my mother gave me as a gift."

"Yes, Bobbie Brown, I had some of that. Frankly, I prefer Estee Lauder. It's cheaper and available everywhere. And how is Chucky?"

"He's fine. Did I tell you he is walking—though it is more like he is running on the balls of his feet. Jules say he thinks he is going to grow up to be a track star."

"How do you like motherhood? I think I would like to get married someday, but I am not sure I want to have children. They are so demanding on your time."

"That's certainly true, but being a mother makes you feel you are doing something important—contributing to the flow of life." Jennifer paused, then added: "If you meet the right man, Kimberly, you will just want to have his baby. Anyway, that is how I feel."

"Men, oh yes, the ones I have met lately are all such a bunch of jerks. They want to fit you into their routines. If they are physicians, they want to sandwich you between their patients and golf. I don't want to be a third string wife. If I can't be number one, forget it!"

"Well, Kimberly, life is filled with compromises. It all depends on what you really want. What are your priorities?"

Oh, did I tell you? I received a promotion at work. I am now an Assistant Director of a project we have with the

CIA, though I'm not supposed to talk about it, but you are my oldest and most trusted friend. You won't say anything to anyone, will you?"

"No, Kimberly, you know you can trust me. We've been friends since we were in grade school. What is your new job?"

"Well, as you know, I work out at the Research Triangle Park. What they want me to do is coordinate the different activities for the new Over-The-Horizons Program. You know about the Drones. We have had them for years, but they are not always successful in finding the right target. You remember how all the wrong people were killed when we were leaving Afghanistan. What we're interested in doing is adding some psychic power to the military team. We have two different types of psychics— those who do distant viewing and those who read the past, present, and future."

"That all sounds very interesting. What is your role?"

"I'm the Coordinator. I'm responsible for making sure all the units work together."

"That certainly sounds like a very important job."

"It really is. We had a team back when Obama was President, remember. The team tracked down and killed Osama bin Laden. Trump, when he became President, disassembled the whole thing. He was such an insecure and paranoid person—thought the CIA might use the psychics to spy on him. Anyway, we are trying to put the team back together again."

"Oh, oh, it sounds like Chucky is waking up from his nap. I had better go and check on him."

"One more thing—the real reason I called. One of the psychics, who is a member of our team, is going to deliver a talk at the Enlightenment Center in Durham next week. I'm going and I would like to take you as my guest."

"I don't know. What would I do with Chucky? It isn't easy to find a babysitter."

"Bring him with us. I would like to see how he has grown. It would do both of you good get out of the house for a change. And who knows, Madam Monet might even be able to tell you something important about your future."

....

Chucky Stein was at the top of his game. That morning his mother had fed him his favorite breakfast of warm cereal and apple sauce, which was followed by a bath. When he was dry, his mother had dressed him in his new blue and white sailor suit. She even put a curl in the hair on top of his head. Yes, Chucky Stein felt loved and at one with the world.

After his mother showered, put on her makeup, and dressed, a lady came to the front door of the apartment. She

184

talked with his mother for a few minutes. Then his mother got his coat from the closet, and they all three left the apartment and got into the lady's car.

Chucky had been seated on his mother's lap rather than in his usual car seat. The car stopped in front of a large house he had never seen before. There were people gathered in front of the house. They all looked at him when he got out of the car—some smiled and reached out to touch him. He was not sure how he felt about being around all of those new people, but he held tightly to his mother's hand as they walked through the front door of the house.

Once they were inside the house, there were even more people. They were all seated on chairs scattered around the room. The lady who had driven them to the house found two chairs, one for herself and another for his mother. Chucky, as was often the case, found himself seated on his mother's lap.

Shortly, a woman with long, dark hair stood up and waved her hand in the air. All the other people in the room stop talking and turned to face the woman. Chucky was not sure why, but big people like his mother and father liked to listen to other people talk. Now, he said to himself, would be a good time to settle down in his mother's lap and take a nap.

When Chucky awakened, all the people in the room were standing and clapping. The woman with the dark hair was standing in front of a large window and hugging other people. There was a warm, friendly feeling in the room. He guessed all these people knew and liked one another and that they had been here before.

Finally, after most of the people had left the room, the lady who had brought Chucky and his mother to the house walked over to the lady with dark hair and began speaking with her. After a short time, both ladies returned to where Chucky and his mother were sitting.

Chucky's mother placed him on the floor when she stood to greet the lady with the dark hair. The two women shook hands and smiled at one another. The lady with the dark hair bent over and stroked Chucky on the head. It was then that Chucky saw the bright object the lady wore around her neck. As it swung in his direction, he caught hold of it with both hands. It was hard and cold to the touch. All three women laughed, while his mother pried the object free from his grip.

Finally, the lady who had driven them to the house said something about taking Chucky out back to see some puppies. Puppies! There was a word Chucky knew and was interested in. The lady took Chucky by the hand and exited the back door—leaving his mother and the lady with the dark hair standing together. Outside on the grass there were a number of furry puppies playing with one another. Chucky was no sooner down the steps than he joined in the game of chase.

After Chucky and the puppies were tired of playing, the lady took him back inside the house. His mother and the lady with the dark hair were sitting together. The lady had her arm around his mother's shoulder. All the warmth had drained out of the room, leaving it strained and cold. His mother kept touching her eyes and nose with a piece of soft paper. What had the lady said to his mother that had changed the mood of the whole day?

....

The feel of fall was heavy in the air. Gone were the oppressive heat and humanity of summer. There was a hint of cool dampness in the breeze. The kind of dampness that tells you it is time to put away summer clothing and to rummage around for last year's sweaters. Yellow-brown leaves scurried across the ground—leaving the feeling that winter could not be far behind

Jennifer had been hurrying around the apartment all afternoon. She had dressed Chucky in his long-sleeve shirt and warm sweater. Then she had dashed into the kitchen to pick up a bag of dry bread crumbs. Returning to the living room, she picked up Chucky and hurried out the front door of the apartment, leaving her iPhone on the kitchen counter.

Placing Chucky in his stroller, Jennifer walked quickly down the sidewalk leading from her apartment to the east gate of Duke University Gardens. Passing through the heavy steel gate, she and Chucky picked their way down the path leading to the rose garden. The last rays of the sun touched the remaining petals casting off a soft glow of whites, yellows, and reds. Jennifer stopped to admire a particularly large white rose. She was tempted to pick it and take it home, but she had been too well-bred to give in to such urges.

Leaving the rose garden behind, Jennifer and Chucky headed down the cinder path leading to the gazebo.

In the spring the path had been lined with delicately colored pansies, but now they were all out of season. Their beds were neatly spaded and carefully lined with pine straw— waiting next year's planting. At the end of the cinder path stood the gazebo—a steel structure fashioned in the shape of a half-sphere. Jennifer and Chucky passed through the gazebo and carefully worked the stroller down the rough steps. What lay before them was their destination—the goldfish pond.

Earlier that day Jennifer had agreed to meet Jules at the pond just before dusk. They had made the same arrangement many times before. Jules would finish his research at the library; then they would all meet at the pond and watch Chucky feed the fish as they jump out of the water fighting for the bread crumbs. The sun was heavy in the sky when Jennifer and Chucky settled on a big rock to wait for Jules.

Jules was slow to arrive at the goldfish pond. Never mind, he had been late many times before, delayed in the library. Jennifer and Chucky grew tired of waiting. They open the bag of bread crumbs and began feeding the goldfish. Chucky eagerly stuck his hand in the bag and threw the bread crumbs to the fish. He loved to see the little fish darting around in the pond—golden streaks against the dark green of the moss and lily pads. Chucky held out his hand for more bread crumbs. The little goldfish jumped and splashed, trying to beat one another to the crumbs. Chucky squealed with excitement and held out his hand for more crumbs.

Jennifer gazed across the pond at the flower garden. It was such a lovely garden. She hoped to have one like it someday when Jules finished his work at the university. The colors were not as bright as they had been in the spring, but the fire bushes were clearly coming into their own. She hoped to have some of those in her garden too. It was such a nice place to bring Chucky—so calm—so peaceful—so friendly.

Turning her attention back to the fish pond, Jennifer helped Chucky break off little pieces of bread and throw them to the goldfish. She hardly noticed as the shadows of evening were growing heavy on the garden—creating strange and eerie images in the murky waters. Suddenly as she was gazing down into the dark waters of the pond, she thought she saw the reflection of someone in the pond—a young woman who appeared to be standing behind her and peering over her shoulder. Jennifer turned, prepared to offer the woman a friendly greeting. To her surprise, however, there was no one there. Jennifer looked quickly around the pond. There was no one anywhere to be seen—just herself and Chucky—alone—all alone in the garden. A feeling of uneasiness came flooding over her. She wanted to get up and leave—take Chucky and head for home. But she had promised Jules she would wait for him at the fish pond. Where was Jules? What was taking him so long? Jennifer looked around the garden once more. No one—there was no one in sight. Had she been mistaken? Were her eyes playing tricks on her? It must have been only the shadows of the pines. Surly that was it. Jennifer gathered up her courage and looked back once more into the pond.

The waters in the pond were no longer friendly and peaceful. They were wild and violent—filled with darting shadows. Jennifer gazed down into the shifting images hoping against hope not to see what she had seen before. Yet there it was again—appearing out of the dark shadows of the pond. There was no mistaking it. It was really there—there in the pond. Jennifer looked straight into the face of the young woman. Her features were as clear as if she were looking into a mirror—deep set eyes—a pained expression around her mouth. She was holding out her hands—reaching out toward Jennifer and Chucky.

Jennifer's heart jumped, pounded wildly. A cold numbness started in her hands but quickly spread throughout her body. Jennifer braced herself and glanced quickly back into the dark waters of the pond. The reflection was still there—looking up at her with yearning eyes. Her hands were beckoning Jennifer and Chucky to join her in the murky waters of the pond.

Jennifer's anxiety turned to panic. Nothing like this had ever happened to her in her life—not in her wildest dreams. Dreams—yes—that must be it. She was dreaming. Maybe—if she concentrated really hard—tried to awaken—she would find she was home in bed safe in Jules' arms. Where was Jules? What was taking him so long? No, it was not a dream. She was not at home. She and Chucky were at Duke University Gardens. This terrible experience was all real! Jennifer got up quickly from where she and Chucky had been sitting next to the fish pond. Her sudden motion startled Chucky, who began to cry. The bag of bread crumbs fell into the water—sending the little goldfish scurrying in all directions.

Jennifer could think of only one thing—leaving the garden as quickly as possible—leaving and going home to safety—leaving this weird world far behind and returning to one of normality. Jennifer had forgotten all about Jules. She was taking her baby and going home the same way she had come. Buckling Chucky securely into his stroller—her heart filled with confusion and dread—she took her crying little boy on a wild ride up the rocky steps that led to the gazebo. The gazebo was now a dark and unfriendly place. The twisted vines that laced its steel structure seemed to come to life—reaching out and trying to snatch her baby away from her. The whole garden, which had always seemed like such a peaceful place, was suddenly transformed into a dark and foreboding world.

Jennifer hurried along the cinder path leading to the rose garden—trying to reassure herself and her crying baby that everything was going to be all right. She could only think of one thing—getting out of the garden and returning home as quickly as possible. The woods were dark and mysterious. Her imagination played free rein with her fantasies. She saw shadowy figures lurking behind every rock and tree—hoping, just hoping she would slip and fall.

This time Jennifer did not stop to admire the remaining roses in the garden. All she saw were thorns—long spiny arms reaching out—trying to catch and tear her flesh—trying to snatch Chucky away from her as he bounced around in his stroller.

Leaving the rose garden, Jennifer hurried up the flight of rock steps—almost losing control of the stroller and dumping Chucky on the ground. Finally, the heavy steel gate to the garden was in sight. Soon—very soon—

she would be home—home safe from all the strange happening in the garden.

Jennifer took the last rocky steps and raised her eyes—looking at the heavy steel gate. Her heart stopped. A frozen sob stuck in her throat. The massive steel gate was closed, locked shut. Panic took possession of her soul. Pushing Chucky's stroller in a mad dash, she came to the gate and pressed herself firmly against it—hoping— praying a miracle would happen and something would open the gate. It was all to no avail. The darkness suddenly enveloped her feelings—turning panic to despair. The forces of darkness called out against her: "Trapped, Jennifer, you're trapped!"

Suddenly a hand from out of nowhere reached out and grabbed her by the arm. Jennifer screamed, felt faint. Her hands slipped from the handle on the stroller. What would happen to her—to Chucky?

"What's the matter?" Jules asked, steadying his wife's collapsing figure. "Why didn't you wait for me at the goldfish pond?"

....

Jules stein was in his element. He loved to lecture—particularly when it was to a captive audience of students who were engaged in taking notes for a promised examination. And the topic of the day was one of Jules' favorites—common misunderstandings about the Constitution. Glancing at his watch, Jules could see he was just about out of time. One more example, he thought, just one more.

"I was watching the news the other evening on CNN. They were reporting on a member of the House of Representatives in Washington. A Representative had claimed the 2nd Amendment was written to arm citizens so they could overthrow the government if it ever fell into the hands of a tyrant." Jules looked intently at his students. "Fiction, pure unadulterated fiction!" That isn't what the 2nd Amendment says? Who can find its wording in one of their textbooks?"

The students began looking around the room to see if anyone had brought a textbook to class. Blank faces told him that most had not. Presently, a hand went up from a young woman seated in the middle of the room.

"Yes, Sandra, would you read it for us?"

Sandra began to read: "A well regulated Militia, being necessary for the security of a free State, the right of the people to keep and bear arms, shall not be infringed."

"Thank you Sandra. Where is the stuff about overthrowing tyrants? It is not in there, explicitly or implicitly. What do the words practically mean?" Jules looked around the room, which was filled with blank faces. "Ok, let me put it another way. Why did the Founding Fathers bother to write the 2nd Amendment? What purpose or end was it designed to serve?"

A hand went up in the back of the room.

"Yes, Michael."

"Everyone was given the right to own a gun."

"Yes and no. During the colonial period, guns were expensive and hard to come by. No more than ten percent of the population owned a gun. On top of that guns did not work very well. Your flint and powder had to be dry. Again, let me ask: What was its purpose? Look at the words in the first half of the Amendment. What do they say?

Sandra voluntarily offered: "It says a well regulated Militia is necessary for the security of a free State."

"Great! There is the statement of purpose—to create a militia. But why have a militia? Because they did not want to fork out the cash to support a standing army. It was cheaper to have a militia and to have them bring their guns with them if there was going to be a skirmish. America was to be defended by an army of citizen-soldiers. At least that was the upfront argument. The Founders, however, didn't give us the real reason they wanted a militia. All the southern states were populated by thousands of slaves. Slavery was a cruel and brutal institution. We have all read about the Nat Turner Rebellion. It was just one of hundreds. Southern Whites lived in constant fear of a slave revolt. Who would quell the riot? Why the militia of course. The 2nd Amendment was an instrument of slavery—how to keep Black folk picking cotton. In my humble opinion, it should have been abolished by the 13th Amendment." Jules glanced down at his watch. "I see our hour is up. Time flies when you are having fun. Check and see what your texts say about the 2nd Amendment. I'll see you next week.

Jules began gathering up his notes from the desk when he noticed that Mike McDonald, the football player, was still seated at his desk. Jules settled himself in the desk next to Mike's and asked: "Is there something I can help you with?"

Mike smiled, shook his head. "No, not really, I just wanted to speak with you for a minute. I wanted you to know how much I'm enjoying your class. I don't always understand all you are talking about—like just now on the 2nd Amendment—but I remember all your stories."

"Well, thanks Mike, I enjoy having you in class too."

"How are you coming with your research on the Devil's Tramping Ground?"

"How do you know about that?"

"Oh, the students always know what their professors are working on, scuttlebutt."

"I see, you are all a bunch of sleuths."

"The Devil's Tramping Ground is an interesting place. My friends and I drove out there a few weeks ago. We took along a 12 pack of beer and some weed. It wasn't easy finding the place in the dark, but we located the circle and settled down to have a few beers. Dick, you haven't met him, he is the guy who furnished the weed. It was pretty great stuff. We all smoked more than we should have—considering we had to drive home. After we had finished the 12 pack and smoked up all the weed, we said goodbye to the Devil and started back down the trail. I brought up the rear. At some point, I turned around to take a final look at the place, and you won't believe what I saw. It was like a hologram—you know—something straight out of Star Wars. There was a bonfire right where we had been standing a few minutes earlier—someone was crumpled on the ground—guys were standing around the fire—several dogs were tied to a tree. I couldn't believe my eyes. I turned and called to my friends who were farther down the trail—but when I turned to look again the scene had changed. What do you think? Was I seeing things? Had I smoked too much pot? I don't know. What do you think?

....

Jennifer had been scurrying around the kitchen all afternoon baking cookies for Halloween. She had always loved baking cookies. Her mother said she must have acquired her love of baking from her grandmother. Jennifer's clearest memories of her grandmother were ones where the two of them were baking cookies together. Her grandmother had show Jennifer how to mix the dough from scratch—mixing together just the right measures of flour, milk, salt, sugar, and baking soda. Too much or too little of any would ruin the texture of the dough. Then how to roll out the dough using an old fashioned wooden rolling pin. When the dough was just right in terms of thickness, they used an ancient collection of tin cookie cutters to give individuality to each cookie. Jennifer's favorite cutters were the star, the dog, the house, and of course the little gingerbread man. Her grandmother had given her all of the cutters before she died. They were among Jennifer's most prized possessions.

Chucky was excited too. He knew something special was coming. His mother had been busy all week sewing and fitting him with a costume that was warm and fuzzy. It was white with a round stubby tail. There was also a hood that came up over his head leaving only his face showing. The hood had long floppy ears that kept falling in front of his face. Finally his mother pinned them so they stood straight up on top of his head. Chucky loved being a rabbit.

Children in brightly colored costumes had been ringing the door bell—calling out trick-or-treat—streaming into the apartment and collecting Jennifer's cookies all evening. Chucky laughed at all of the funny costumes. He enjoyed seeing all of the other children who lived in the neighborhood. Jennifer was pleased to see how the children couldn't wait to begin munching down on her cookies.

Late in the evening, after all of the other trick-or-treaters had gone home, there came a loud rapping on the door. Jennifer and Chucky open the door and were greeted by six little children who were dressed like Duke Blue Devils. Jennifer could not help thinking how some mother had really gone overboard—sewing six children's costumes for Halloween. The children were accompanied by a witch with a crooked nose. They all came barging through the front door and into the living room where they broke into a chorus of trick-or-treat. Jennifer smiled and gave each child one of her remaining cookies. Then the strangest thing happened. Rather than leaving like all of the other children, the witch and the little devils formed a circle around Jennifer and Chucky and began chanting something in a foreign language. The witch, who was standing right in front of Jennifer, stuck her left hand in front of Jennifer's face. Jennifer looked carefully at the witch's hand . . . something was terribly wrong. The witch's hand had an extra finger. Jules had told her about a group of villagers who lived in an isolated valley in Spain who had an extra finger on one hand. Could the witch be from Spain?

Suddenly the chanting stopped and the witch and the little devils clasp hands and began skipping around in a circle. They made a whirring sound like an electric motor as they went spinning around and around. Once, twice . . . six times they revolved around Jennifer and Chucky. When they finally stopped, the witch used her six fingered hand to form an image in the air resembling a tornado or whirlpool. Then she blew her swirling creation in the direction of Jennifer and Chucky. Jennifer found herself standing in the center of what resembled a dust devil. Chucky coughed and buried his face in his mother's shoulder. Jennifer closed her eyes—trying not to breath. When the swirling air finally stopped, Jennifer opened her eyes. To her amazement the witch and the six little Duke Blue Devils had all vanished out the front door. She would later ask herself: What message was the witch trying to deliver—six little blue devils, six fingers on her left hand, six times around in a spinning circle? And what was the significance of the number 666?

....

Jules found himself knocking on the frame of the open office door. The man inside the office turned in his swivel chair to greet him. "I wonder if I could have a few minutes of your time."

"Sure, Jules, come on in. What brings you over to this side of the campus?"

"Well, Professor Chillcott, I've run into a bit of a problem with my research."

"Is that all," Chillcott replied with a bit of a chuckle. "Writing a dissertation is never easy. How to satisfy all the members of your committee can be a real pain. I remember it took me three years to finish mine— and that was back in the good-old-days. How are you coming on the Devil's Tramping Ground?"

"That's exactly it. You recommended I should contact Professor Davidson over at Chapel Hill. Well, he helped me run a seismic test on the Devil's Tramping Ground. We used a few sticks of dynamite to get a reading. Based on what he saw on the seismograph, he found an anomaly in the data. He told me he thought there might be something buried near the surface inside the circle, and I might want to dig a few test holes just to find out."

"Good, Davidson is an excellent scholar. I would trust his judgment. Did you dig the holes?"

"Yes, that's what I wanted to talk with you about. In the last hole I was working on—down about four feet—I uncovered a human skull. What should I do with or about it?"

"Did you leave the skull where you found it?"

"Yes, I wanted to talk with you before I did or said anything."

"That was smart. I'm going to tell you something which should remain just between the two of us. Are we agreed?"

"Yes, of course."

"How many years do you plan on staying at Duke and working on your dissertation?"

"I hoped to finish sometime in the next year."

"Good, keep that goal in mind," Professor Chillcott said, leaning forward in his chair—an earnest expression on his face. "Then go back to your holes and cover them all up. Don't say anything to anyone about finding some old bones. This may sound like strange advice coming from an archaeologist who has spent a life digging around for old bones, but it is the best advice I have to offer you. If you call the county sheriff's office, they will want to send out a forensic team. They will want to know why you were digging in the Devil's Tramping Ground. Do you know anything about the person whose skull you found? They will publish an announcement in the local paper. Then all hell will break loose! Everyone will want to know whose DNA is the old bones. The NAACP will want to know if it was a Black person hanged by the KKK. The Clan will want to know if it was one of their own. The Native American Association will want to know if it was one of their people. And you my friend," Professor Chillcott gave Jules an earnest look, "will be stuck right in the middle of it. Do you have the time to deal with all of those people— perhaps for years?'

Jules shook his head, replied: "Hell no!"

"Then be smart—go out there and cover up all those holes—keep your mouth shut about what you've found!"

....

Jennifer and Chucky knocked loudly on the old weather-beaten door, knocked and waited. It seemed like forever before they heard footsteps coming to the door. "Hello, Addie, I'm sorry to have to drop in on you like this, but we were out this way and Chucky ran out of milk." She held out an empty bottle. "I wonder if we could borrow some from you."

Addie smiled, replied: "Well, just don't stand there. Come on in out of the cold. I should have some milk in the icebox."

Jennifer and Chucky followed Addie into the kitchen. It was a large, cheerful room—the kind of kitchen they used to build when women spent the better part of their lives preparing meals for large families. The kitchen was heated with a large wood burning stove. Across from the stove was a row of painted cupboards. In the middle of the kitchen was a heavy oak table, which had been used for a cutting board for meat as well as a level place for mixing dough for baking bread. The refrigerator sat in a small alcove just off from the kitchen. It too was of ancient vintage.

Addie took a quart of milk out of the refrigerator and filled Chucky's bottle. "Would you like it warmed?"

"No, he takes it cold."

Chucky took his bottle in both hands and began to squirm to get down on the floor. He toddled across the floor in the direction of the stove.

"Don't let him touch the stove," Addie cautioned. "It's hot."

Jennifer quickly headed Chucky off from the stove and pointed him in a different direction.

"I see he is walking," Addie observed. "He's really grown since you were out here rummaging through the attic."

"Yes, the last time I took him to the doctor he weighed 30 pounds."

"Walking," Addie mused, "why haven't you weaned him? If they're big enough to walk, they are old enough to wean."

Jennifer looked embarrassed by Addie's question. "Well, I know, I should have weaned him by now, but he likes his bottle so much, and it is convenient and easy. Maybe we'll give it another try after Christmas."

Addie shook her head. "You're going to spoil that child. I raised one spoiled child and look where he is today—sitting in prison. You don't do your children any favor by spoiling them."

"We'd better be getting back. Jules will be wondering what happened to us. He is over at the Devil's

Tramping Ground. It is all part of his research. Perhaps you heard some dynamite going off a few weeks ago. Jules and a professor from Chapel Hall were running a scientific test."

"Dynamite!" Addie's eyes grew large. "Did I hear some dynamite? I thought it was going to shake this old house down. Since then we've had nothing but trouble around here. The chickens stopped laying eggs, and the ground still shakes from time to time. A big hole opened up behind the barn. The pig fell into the hole, and we had to tie a rope around him and use the tractor to pull him out. Dynamite! I don't want nothing to do with no dynamite."

"I'll tell Jules what you said. I'm sure he doesn't know anything about that."

"I don't like it—dynamite—that baby at the Devil's Tramping Ground. Why don't you leave him here with me. You and your husband can pick him up on your way back to the city." She gave Chucky a warm smile. "We'd do just fine together, wouldn't we?"

Jennifer hesitated for a moment—worried about what Jules would think. She had already been gone too long. "No, Chucky will be fine. Jules isn't setting off anymore dynamite. He covering up some holes he dug." She hesitated for a minute—could she tell Addie about the bones. Surely it would be alright. Addie wasn't about to tell anyone. "While Jules was digging, he came across some old bones. He asked one of his professors what to do about them, and he told Jules to cover them up. I'm sure you won't say anything to anyone about them."

Addie gave Jennifer a hard, worrisome look. "Bones, old bones," shaking her head, she added: "Black folk always said that place was cursed."

....

Jennifer slipped Chucky into his winter coat with the furry collar and zipped it up tight. Then she started up the path leading to the Devil's Tramping Ground. Her arms were heavy with Chucky, who was stilling holding on to his bottle of milk. Jennifer's mind was a swirl—overflowing with conflicting thoughts and feelings. Something Addie had said triggered an avalanche of emotions. Cursed—that place was cursed! What an ugly word. Where had she heard that word before? Madam Monet had used the word—said her family had been cursed a long time ago. Were curses real? She had read about the Kennedy family having been cursed. Look at what had happened to John and Bobby! Could it be true? Had her family really been cursed?

What about the moles she and Chucky shared? Were they signs of the curse? What about the face of the young woman in the goldfish pond? Why didn't the

Halloween witch simply leave the apartment? And what in the world was the significance of the number 666? Was it all part of some mysterious curse?

Jennifer hardly noticed the bog as she carried Chucky across. Should she tell Jules about her thoughts? What would he say? Would he tell her she had a vivid imagination—that it was all superstition? One thing was for sure—she and Chucky were never coming back to this place again. It was spooky; she hated it. She would tell Jules her thoughts on the matter, perhaps later.

When Jennifer and Chucky arrived at the circle, Jules was just finishing raking the dirt he had dug out of the holes. The afternoon sun was low in the sky—just touching the tops of the big pines. The smell of a wood burning fireplace was in the air. The forest was strangely silent— except for the distant baying of a hound. Jennifer felt a sudden chill; she pulled her baby tightly against her breasts. This would be the last time she would ever come to the Devil's Tramping Ground. She was certain about that.

"Hi, Honey, glad to see you're back. I was about ready to send out the Hound of Baskerville to look for you. I'm about finished here. The winter rains will smooth out where I was digging. How was Addie?"

"Oh, she's fine. She gave us some milk for Chucky's bottle. She told me that when you set off the dynamite it had upset her chickens. They stopped laying eggs."

Jules laughed. "Upset her chickens. That's rich. I'll have to remember and share that story with Professor Davidson. I'll bet I could fill up the pages of a dissertation with all the superstitions Addie carries around in her head."

Jennifer's iPhone rang—holding Chucky with both hands made it impossible to answer. "Jules, would you mind taking Chucky for a minute while I take this call?" She held Chucky out for his father to take.

Jules dropped his rake in the middle of the circle and walked to where Jennifer was holding Chucky. Bouncing his son a few times in his arms and giving him a big kiss on the cheek, Jules returned to where he had left his tools in the middle of the circle.

Jennifer looked down at her iPhone. The call was from Madam Monet. She had given her the number at their meeting at the Enlightenment House. What could she possibly want? "Hello," Jennifer said politely, "I'm surprised and delighted to hear from you. I hoped to speak with you again. So much has happened in my life since we last spoke." Jennifer listened carefully to what Madam Monet was saying. "Oh, Chucky, he's fine—he's right here with Jules and me." She listened again—answered: "We're out at the Devil's Tramping Ground. Jules is covering up some holes he dug." Madam Monet continued talking.

"Time of great danger for Chucky—yes, we'll watch him like a hawk. We'll be going home soon."

While Jennifer was talking, Jules stood Chucky on the ground while he gathered up his tools and moved them to the beginning of the trail. No sooner had he stepped outside the circle than there was a sudden shaking of the earth. The quake was sufficiently violent that Jules had to steady himself with the rake. Turning around he saw Chucky sitting on the ground—having dropped his bottle—a bewildered look on his face. Holding out his arms toward his father, Chucky spoke his first word, "Dada."

And then—in the blink of an eye—the unimaginable happened. A large white dog suddenly appeared from out of nowhere—jumped into the middle of the circle—snatched Chucky up by the furry collar on his coat—cleared the outer parameter of the circle in a single bound. No sooner were Chucky and the dog outside the circle than the ground inside the circle simply opened its mouth and swallowed itself in a single gulp—uncovering a black pit descending down, down, down into the bowls of the earth—exposing a maelstrom of swirling nothingness.

Jennifer dropped her iPhone and hurried to where the dog was licking Chucky's face. Jules knelt down and began stroking the dog's head and ears. He checked its leather collar, which had a bright metal plate attached. The dog's name was clearly etched on the plate, **Basker.**

The End

Made in the USA
Monee, IL
31 January 2022